THE DESERT

Bryon Morrigan

DarkHart Press
Ward Hill, MA

THE DESERT
by
Bryon Morrigan

© 2007 Bryon Morrigan. All Rights Reserved.

This is a work of fiction. Names, characters, places and incidents are products of the author's imagination or are used fictitiously. Any resemblance to actual events, locales, persons is entirely coincidental. No part of this book may be reproduced in any form or by any means, electronic or mechanical, including photocopying, recording or by any information storage and retrieval systems, without the written permission of the copyright owner.

ISBN10: 0-9787318-6-7

ISBN 13: 978-0-9787318-6-1

Cover art:
Front Cover: Peter Szmer
Back cover: D. Michael Ringer
Design/Concept: Pam Marin-Kingsley

Published in 2007
by
Darkhart Press
PO Box 8009
Ward Hill, MA 01835

For my best friend and ideal reader,
Shai,
and also to
the most wonderful children in the world,
Gretchen and Gwendolyn,
who always enjoy
my *'smooky'* stories.

PART ONE

The Journal of Specialist Forbes

Chapter 1

The Desert. 22 October 2009. 1016 Hours.

"Take us as close as possible to the base of that hill, Densler," said the Army officer. He lowered his binoculars, stepped back into the Humvee, and closed the door.

"Yes, Sir," replied Specialist Densler, his driver. Densler was becoming mildly perturbed with Captain Henderson's fixation for checking out every little anomalous geographical feature. It was quite obvious to Densler that the Captain was hoping to find some kind of mass grave, weapon of mass destruction, or secret terrorist training facility. Densler often joked to his buddies that the Captain was after a "War Crime Merit Badge." The thought of what such a badge might look like caused Densler to smile in spite of himself.

Densler put the truck in low gear and took a sharp right turn off road, toward the lone hill. He could see what had piqued Henderson's interest. Near the summit, there was an outcropping of rocks that looked like they might be shielding a small cave. It also looked like it was going to be a hard climb up there, though.

Goddamnit, he thought. *Yeah, I'm sure that Saddam buried a few hundred Kurds up there. In fact, I'll bet that he personally lugged a few Scud missiles up the hill. Better yet, he chose this spot for an insurgency training camp. Great idea, being that there's no sign of water or supplies for a bajillion miles.*

Of course, Densler didn't vocalize any of these objections. Like most soldiers, he had learned to keep his mouth shut and do his duty. He wasn't happy that he'd been stuck in this godforsaken country for nearly three years now. It didn't matter that he was angry that the military had never found any significant caches of nuclear or biological weapons. It didn't matter that he thought the entire war was a load of crap. Specialist Densler was a soldier, and for him that was the only thing that mattered.

At the base of the hill, Densler stopped the Humvee and exited the vehicle. Captain Henderson followed suit and began pulling out equipment they might need: flashlights, rope, water.

Densler looked at the hill. *Great,* he thought. *It's even worse up close. It looks like the whole hill is practically nothing but rock. This will be just peachy to climb. Just friggin' peachy.*

"After you, Sir," said Densler, silently chuckling to himself.

Captain Henderson started ascending the rocky hill, heading towards the peculiar formation near the top. Densler followed behind, picking his footing, which slowed his pace down slightly.

About halfway up, the Captain slipped on a patch of small rocks and fell hard on his side. He picked himself up and tried to regain his dignity.

"Watch your footing up here, Specialist," he called down to Densler, "It gets trickier as you get higher."

Actually, thought Densler, *it's just the same as the rest of the hill. Just worry about your own self, Sir.*

After nearly twenty minutes of climbing, the two soldiers reached the rocky anomaly. Large boulders clumped together on the side of the hill, and a huge flat rock projected out of the hill above them, creating a sort of roof-like structure. Beneath the flat rock, there was utter darkness.

The Captain pulled the flashlights from his rucksack and handed one to Densler. Then he flipped his on and aimed it at the darkness. It barely pierced the black recess.

"Holy shit," said Henderson. "It's bigger than I thought in there." He stepped forward to investigate.

Densler followed behind, shining his flashlight around, trying to locate the walls to either side. He thought he saw some graffiti on the left wall and went to investigate.

He shined the cheap Army flashlight at the wall, but it was too dim for him to make out the characters until he got closer. It looked liked English writing.

"Sir?" said Densler. "I think you'd better see this."

"What is it, Specialist?"

"I think we aren't the first Americans to find this place."

"Damn it," said Henderson. He walked over to where Densler was inspecting the wall.

No chance of finding anything worth shit in here now, thought Densler. He smiled.

Densler pointed to some graffiti written on the rock wall that looked to have been scraped in the rock and then drawn over with a thick black marker to make it more noticeable.

THE DESERT

Henderson read the message out loud, "Here lies SPC Forbes, last surviving member of 4th Platoon, 3rd Squadron, 66th ACR. May God have mercy on your souls." Next to the message, a large arrow pointed into the deep recesses of the cave.

"That's pretty morbid, Sir," said Densler.

"Wait a sec, Densler," said Henderson. "Fourth platoon? Sixty-sixth armored cav regiment? Those were the guys that disappeared during the invasion."

"Eight Up Platoon?" said Densler. "Shit!"

"This doesn't make sense though. They were supposed to be hundreds of miles away from here. They couldn't have been *that* lost."

"Do you want me to check out the rest of the cave, Sir?" asked Densler. Suddenly, this mission had become interesting.

"No...Yeah...I'll come with you."

The cave itself was not particularly wide, maybe thirty feet at the mouth and it funneled inwards as they explored it further. About a hundred feet into the cave, it came to a sort of cul-de-sac and ended. On the floor were the remnants of Specialist Forbes' camp, as well as the remains of the soldier himself.

"Jesus," said Densler.

The desiccated remains of the soldier lay on a tattered sleeping bag on the rock floor. The dry desert air had caused the body to shrivel up and mummify.

Next to the body, the soldiers found a pit that Forbes had obviously used for a campfire. Scattered around the room were various bits of military equipment. Densler found a Kevlar helmet, an M-16 rifle, and even some radio equipment that appeared to have been pulled out of a Humvee.

Off to the right, he found a rock with an almost horizontal face, which looked to have been used as a desk. A small journal had been placed upon the rock. It was sitting as close to the center of the rock face as one could be discerned. An assortment of pens and pencils were laid neatly next to the journal.

"Sir?" said Densler. He picked up the journal, and carefully opened the cover and looked inside. "You might want to look at this," he said, handing it to the officer.

"Hot damn," whispered the Captain. "He wrote a fucking diary. I'll be briefing General Franklin before the day is over."

Densler rolled his eyes behind the officer's back. "Now what, Sir?" he said. "Should we go back down and call this in?" He watched Henderson scanning the manuscript, eyes glued to the pages.

"Yeah," the captain said without interest. "I guess we better go call Headquarters."

Half and hour later, the two soldiers were back in the Humvee and ready to go. Densler tried the radio, but could get nothing but static.

"Well I guess that solves one mystery, Sir," said Densler. "We know why he couldn't call for help. I can't get any kind of signal out here at all. I've never seen anything like it."

"Well," said Henderson. "Let's get moving anyway. You can keep trying as we head towards HQ. In the meantime, I'm going to start seeing if I can make sense of this manuscript before we get there."

"Yes, Sir," said Densler. He started up the Humvee and turned back in the direction they had come from. "Sir?" **he** said Densler.

"Yes, Specialist?"

THE DESERT

"GPS isn't working either. I didn't notice before because we weren't following any particular course."

"Can you get us back to HQ without it?"

"Maybe."

"Just do your best," said Henderson. He started reading as soon as the vehicle was in motion. Densler began to wonder about the manuscript.

Maybe when Henderson is done, he thought, *I can get a look at that thing. I mean, it's probably nothing, but I have to admit to being a little curious. They probably just did something stupid, since they did have a history of that, but how the hell do you disappear out here? This isn't World War II! We have global positioning, and satellite radios, and crap like that. How much of an idiot do you actually have to be?*

Chapter 2

Journal Entry One: 1 APR 2003

This is the war diary of SPC David Forbes. If you are reading this, I am probably dead. I make this claim knowing that I would probably never willingly show my private thoughts to another person, so if I am not dead, then it is highly likely that this diary has been stolen, pilfered, or otherwise nefariously exploited by my fellow servicemen. Enjoy.

Sunsets are grander in the desert, you know. In fact, there is a great deal about this country that is completely different from the way that we Americans expect.

For example, I really expected it to be hotter here. Seriously. I grew up in South Florida, so I know what hot, stinky, humid weather is like. Hell, Iraq has nothing on Florida. This place is much milder than a summer in Naples, Florida, my hometown.

Don't get me wrong. Come midday, this place is pretty damned hot. But here, I can wear a full set of military fatigues (BDUs, we call them...) and a flak jacket and still be more comfortable than I'd be in Naples

THE DESERT

wearing a t-shirt and shorts. It's hot, all right, but the humidity isn't bad, and it's that damned humidity that will kill you back home.

The best part about the desert though, is nightfall. It gets downright chilly here at night. That makes sleeping a whole lot easier, trust me. Back home, you don't get a break from either the heat or the humidity at night.

It gets pretty fucking dark at night, though. Oh by the way, I hope you don't mind that word, *fuck*. We soldiers say it a lot. Before I joined the Army, I never cursed. Now...I fucking curse all the time. We all do. It's the fucking Army, hooahh!

So anyway, like I said, it's real fucking dark at night. I learned real quick that it was best not to sleep in the tents at night. You want to stay in the SCIF if you can, and not be wandering around in the darkness. Since you can't use your flashlights (as the enemy might see you), you might accidentally walk right into some piano wire, and we Intel pukes just *love* our piano wire. Or better yet, you get up to use the latrine, then spend all night wandering around looking for your tent. And trust me, it's not all that easy to determine which one is *your* tent in the darkness either.

So what I like to do is curl up on the front seat of a five-ton transport truck. Expando-vans we call them, because they have these side things that well, *expand*. The bench seat is not the most comfortable thing in the world, but it does have a few amenities. For example, when you wake up in the morning, you have all these handy mirrors to use while shaving. The passenger's *oh shit* bar also serves as a nice towel rack. The best part is that nobody but skinny little shits like me can actually sleep on those benches, so you don't have to worry about arguing with anyone over them. We have three of these trucks in our unit, and I'm the only one who sleeps in the cab. All the NCOs (Non-commissioned officers, a.k.a. sergeants, in case you didn't know...) sleep on cots under the trucks. There's a good four-foot or so clearance under there. Makes a good little place for a cot.

In fact, right now as I write this I'm sitting in one of those expando-vans. Since as of tomorrow I'll be assigned to a different unit for a little while, I figured this would be as good a time as any to start a journal. This way, if anything interesting happens to me, at least I'll have this account to maybe use to write a book. I've always wanted to write a book.

So anyway, earlier this night I'm walking back towards the SCIF after using the latrine. The sun is setting and it's getting dark. I don't like being caught outside of the SCIF after sunset. Too damned creepy in that pitch-black darkness. Another soldier is walking straight towards me, heading towards the nasty latrine I just left.

As he gets closer, I realize it's not a *he*, but a *she*. It's SPC Morgan, one of the three MPs (Military Police...) that are attached to our beloved little SCIF. She looks a whole lot like that lesbian folk singer, K.D. Lang. She even has the haircut. In fact, rumor has it she *is* a lesbian. She's pretty tough and masculine, so I can believe it.

So that's why I'm taken completely off guard when, just as she's about to pass by me, she grabs me and kisses me hard... like she's Indiana Jones and I'm some chick he just rescued. Then she spins me around, pulling me close like a lover, to turn me towards the setting sun.

THE DESERT

"I just had to share that with someone," she said. "It's so fucking beautiful."

Then, without further ado, she lets go of me and heads over to the abysmal latrine. I'm still standing there in shock, glad that it was so dark that no one could have seen the encounter. I mean, I'm a little guy (five foot six, 110 pounds) but I'd never been handled like that by a *female* before. (By the way, we say female in the Army. It's nice and clinical and keeps us from accidentally saying *girl*.)

It's only then, after I finally recover my wits, that I finally notice for the first time, even though I'd been in this country for weeks, that it is a beautiful fucking sunset.

Chapter 3

The Desert. 22 October 2009. 1102 Hours.

"What the hell is with this guy?" said Henderson out loud.

"Excuse me, Sir?" replied Densler.

"Oh nothing," said Henderson. "This journal, though. The guy writes the most irrelevant things down. I need to know the how and whys of how that platoon ended up dropping off the face of the earth. All I've learned so far is that some lesbian MP kissed him once."

"Indeed, Sir," said Densler.

Oh, you can't see it, Sir, he thought, *but I'm smiling on the inside. I'd kill to hear you briefing General Franklin about a dead soldier's encounter with a lesbian MP. Priceless.*

"Pull over somewhere, Specialist," said Henderson. "I have to take a leak."

Densler pulled the Humvee off of the crude road. The officer hopped out and looked around for a second before doing his thing.

Jesus H. Christ, thought Densler. *How stupid do you have to be to become an officer? First, the dipshit asks me to*

THE DESERT

pull over somewhere on a road that looks like it hasn't seen traffic in years, as if we needed to stay out of someone's way or something. Then, he looks around before finally whipping it out. Was he looking for a tree? I haven't seen a tree all day. And besides, who the fuck is he hiding himself from?

"Densler," said Henderson. "Try the GPS and radio again."

"Yes, Sir,"

Oh yeah, I'll try them again. I can tell what's going on though, Sir. I haven't heard one drop of piss hit the sandy desert floor. I've figured you out, Sir. You're one of those guys who can't piss in urinals because you're too shy to pee around anyone else. We're in the middle of an uninhabited desert, and you've got stage fright because of me. Hot damn! I definitely want this guy leading me into battle.

Densler checked the GPS and found that it was still not receiving any signal. He turned the radio's volume up and scanned for traffic. All he could hear was static.

That's odd, he thought. *This static sounds kind of creepy. It doesn't sound so much like static as an open channel. In fact, it sounds like someone is transmitting the silence of an empty room over the radio.*

"Sir?" he petitioned the officer with the reluctant bladder.

"Yes, Specialist?" Henderson replied, irritated that he still had yet to urinate.

"Does this static sound weird to you?"

Since Henderson was standing about five feet away from the truck's door. Densler turned the volume up to the maximum so the captain could hear it.

"Not particularly, Specialist," he replied.

"It doesn't sound like static," said Densler. "It sounds like someone has an open channel transmitting from somewhere with no ambient noise. If it were actual static, it would be much louder than this."

"Well, try to get the other person to answer you, then," said Henderson, turning back to his previous engagement.

Densler picked up the transmitter and spoke into the microphone. "This is Black-10, over. Do you copy?" There was no response or change in the transmission. He repeated it two times more and received the same outcome.

Then Densler decided to break the rules a little bit. "Listen. I can hear you out there. I know you are listening. Please respond, over."

For a few more seconds, there was no change. Then, there was a sound.

Click!

Densler looked at Henderson and saw the officer craning his head around to look at the radio. Both men wore puzzled expressions. The sound came again, three times in rapid succession.

Click, click, click!

To Densler, it sounded like somebody was running his or her fingernail across the microphone mesh on the transmitting radio. Henderson had a different theory.

"Maybe it's in Morse code?" said the officer.

A few seconds later, there was an even longer succession of clicks. This time it definitely sounded like someone running a fingernail across the transmitter. It sounded frantic this time, like someone was trying to scrape the mesh right off of the microphone. Then, all of a sudden, the transmission ended. Real static flooded the airwaves, and since Densler had turned the volume up to the maximum, the sound of the static was quite loud. The abrupt cacophony of white noise made both men jump slightly, but Captain Henderson was also rewarded by the fact that he no longer had to struggle

THE DESERT

to urinate. At least he was in the *ready* position. It could have been quite embarrassing had the situation occurred while they were in the Humvee.

After finishing, Henderson got back into the Humvee and they started back on their way to headquarters. Densler left the volume up on the radio so they could hear if there were any more strange transmissions.

After about fifteen minutes, Captain Henderson said, "Can you turn that off now? I want to finish reading this journal before we get back to HQ, and that noise is just too much."

"Yes, Sir," replied Densler. *I wouldn't want to disturb your reading time, Sir.*

Chapter 4

Journal Entry Two: 1 APR 2003 (2)

When I got to the SCIF, I had to check in with SPC Morgan's superior, SGT Hall, and show him my clearance before entering. You see, a SCIF (pronounced like '*skiff*'...) is a *Sensitive Compartmented Information Facility*. That means that anyone going inside our little razor-wire clubhouse has to have a Top Secret/SCI clearance, which is pretty fucking hard to get. I'm not going to get into specifics of what kinds of things classify as Top Secret/SCI because I don't want some damn FBI agent knocking on my door, asking me why I'm divulging classified information. Basically, just remember that it's pretty fucking secret. It's not like *Roswell* secret though, so don't ask me where the aliens are because I don't know. Yeah, I know, what a scam.

Anyway, the whole place is pretty impenetrable, and you have to show your ID to one of those three aforementioned MPs to gain access, even though we all know each other pretty well. The MPs have their own little tent set up at the only gap in the piano

THE DESERT

wire fence that surrounds the enclosure. The piano wire is laid down pretty high and deep, stopping everything but the most determined enemy, so the only way into the SCIF is through that MP tent.

That SGT Hall though, jeez! He's our resident freak. The guy's pretty much tattooed everywhere that doesn't show when he's in his Class A uniform. He has a necklace of skulls tattooed around his neck. If he wasn't wearing his uniform, you could see the word *deviant* in big old English letters arching over his stomach. He even has his septum pierced and can put his dog tag chain through it. Sometimes he does that when we're goofing off in the field during a peacetime operation.

Unfortunately, this isn't a peacetime operation. We're in Iraq, and the *shock and awe* part of the invasion just ended. Luckily, being attached to the SCIF means that I get to follow the regiment's command center around. (The colonel likes the SCIF to be firmly attached to his ass...) That means we haven't seen anything but fireworks in the distance so far, which is fine by me at this point.

I'm a little uncomfortable dealing with SGT Hall at this point. I mean, his subordinate just kissed me, but I'm not gonna say shit and I can't really *brag* about the incident. Nor am I gonna go complaining about some chick (Sorry, I mean *female*...) playing *alpha female* with me on the lonely latrine highway. It was such a weird situation that I want to tell someone, but I can't risk being seen as her *bitch* either. The weirdest thing about the whole thing is that it was kind of cool. I'd never have admitted it to those guys. This is the kind of thing that makes me hope that no one ever reads this journal.

Later in the day, I wondered if Morgan really was a lesbian. Maybe she was just some kind of masculine woman. Men can be kind of femme sometimes without actually being gay. Maybe that was her way of showing that she liked me. Maybe she had been working up the courage to do something like that for months and months.

Or maybe she just liked that fucking sunset a lot. I wasn't going to find out, though. Although I didn't know it at the time, I wouldn't be hanging around at the SCIF for much longer.

As soon as I left SGT Hall at the entrance tent, I took off my Kevlar helmet and unbuckled my web gear. Since camouflage netting pretty heavily conceals the SCIF and the only people inside it are Intel geeks, we tend to be a bit more *casual* in our little clubhouse.

I tossed my M-16 rifle into the cab of the truck I sleep in and headed over to the chairs where the rest of my squad usually hangs out. I see my squad leader, Staff Sergeant Kent, talking to the company commander, Major Morrow. Since the major is a bit of a dick and I didn't want to intrude, I decided to walk past them and see if I could find anyone else in my squad. My luck wasn't that good, though.

"Forbes," Kent said, turning to address me. "Just the man we're looking for."

Fucking great, I think. Now what did I do? This can't be good.

"We need to send you on a special mission, Specialist Forbes," said the major, grinning that evil grin he always used when he was

THE DESERT

giving you a shitty assignment that he wanted you to feel honored to carry out.

"Yes sir," I said. I went to parade rest and tried to look less afraid than I really was. I mean, seriously, a *special mission*? Here? I'll say it again: *This can't be good.*

"We're sending our interrogators out with some infantry units on certain special missions," said the major. "I'm attaching you to fourth platoon of third squadron. They are clearing out a small town to the south of us tomorrow. There probably won't be anything important there, but the colonel wants an interrogator there in case there is any intel that can be gathered from the locals. Sergeant Kent here will give you the details." With that, he turned and walked towards his command truck.

I looked at Sergeant Kent with an expression that could only be described as naked despair. "Fourth platoon, Sergeant?" I said. "Eight Up Platoon? On a raid?"

"Calm down, Forbes," said Kent. "They wouldn't be sending a lone Intel E-4 if there was anything important or dangerous about the mission. In fact, seeing as how it's Eight Up Platoon, I can't see that it's anything but a way to get them as far *away* from battle as possible."

Eight up, or *ate up* is military jargon for severely fucked or crazy. Eight Up Platoon earned its nickname before it even landed in Kuwait during the pre-invasion preparation. Supposedly, some of their equipment had been left unsecured in the hold of their C-130 transport plane. Legend has it that the whole lot of it had slid down the center aisle and slammed into their company commander's Humvee, smashing in the headlights. Their equipment had also suffered damage, and they had had to borrow new NVGs (night vision goggles...) from some of the support squadrons.

Later, on the first day of the offensive, their platoon leader, a fresh from the Academy *butter bar* (Second lieutenant... so named because the rank insignia is a gold bar...), got them completely lost and turned around. They ended up launching a raid against the regiment's kitchen, but luckily they realized their error before anyone got hurt.

"It will only be for a week or two, Forbes," Kent was saying, trying to reassure me.

"Yeah," I said. "But given their current record, that's all it will take for them to get me killed."

THE DESERT

Chapter 5

Journal Entry Three: 2 APR 2003

The next morning, I packed up my bags to accompany Eight Up Platoon on its eight up mission in the middle of eight up Iraq. Needless to say I was not in a pleasant mood.

As I carried my stuff out of the SCIF, I noticed Morgan was manning the MP tent. She was reading a fantasy novel, something about *dark elves*. I thought that was a particularly odd thing for a female to be reading. Heck, I was a real geek about science fiction and fantasy books, but even I wouldn't read something as silly as that.

"See you later, Morgan," I said, trying to appear nonchalant.

"Sure thing, Specialist," she replied, not even looking up at me. The fact that she referred to me by my rank and not even by my last name, led me to believe that the previous night's *incident* was just a fluke, a moment's indiscretion, rather than any long disguised infatuation.

I was both relieved and disappointed. I mean, she wasn't my type, so I was glad that I wouldn't have to reject her. On the other hand, my ego was disappointed that she wasn't pining away for me. I wasn't even remotely attracted to her, so I don't know why I cared. I guess that situations like this affect us and change us more than we know. I only hoped I would recognize the person I would be when I returned home from the war. It sounds so cliché, but war really does change people.

Eight Up Platoon had just arrived outside the command headquarters, and I could see their platoon leader speaking with Major Morrow. I mentally recalled a funeral march from one of Wagner's *Nibelung* operas as I walked towards the small convoy that consisted of three *deuce-and-a-half* transport trucks and two Humvees. Hey, we all cope in our own ways.

As I approached the two officers, Major Morrow stepped back. "Well, here's Specialist Forbes," he said. "I have other business to attend to."

As soon as I saw the expression in the young lieutenant's eyes, I knew I would not be greeted warmly.

"A specialist?" he said. "I had expected some sort of noncommissioned officer at the least." He spoke quickly, with a monotonous New England accent that I couldn't place.

I realized there was no comment I could make at this time that would be immune from recrimination, so I kept my mouth shut. The platoon leader, Lieutenant Montgomery, was looking straight down his nose at me, as if examining the value of a piece of used furniture. It was infuriating, but I managed not to betray even a whiff of my feelings of loathing towards the man.

Lieutenant Montgomery was somewhat tall and thin. He had reddish-orange hair and sharp features that were not attractive in

THE DESERT

the least. He also seemed to have a permanent half-scowl etched on his face. Rumor had it that he had no sense of humor except when it concerned the death or suffering of other people. I had just met him and I already hated the bastard.

"Okay then," Montgomery said. "Get in a truck. We haven't got all day."

The third truck was the least crowded, so I squeezed in on a bench next to a group of fairly downcast soldiers.

One of the soldiers looked down at my tanker boots and furrowed his brow. "I thought we were picking up a spook," he said. "This guy's a tanker. What the fuck do we need with a tank driver?"

I sighed. "I *am* a spook, Private," I said to the soldier, a Private Second Class Settipane. "We Intel weenies often try to look like combat grunts so that if we're captured, they don't try to torture our secrets out. I wear tanker boots so the bad guys think I'm just a tank driver."

"Ah," Settipane said, sneering.

I don't get why your average soldier doesn't care for Intel guys. They act like this is some bad cop movie and we're from Internal Affairs. I guess the myth that *bad intelligence* is the primary reason that soldiers get killed is pretty much ingrained upon the military psyche. Truth be told, we give our information to the officers that make decisions. When things go well, they take all the credit. When anything goes wrong, they blame Intel.

It was uncomfortable sitting there in silence with those guys, so I was glad when the trucks' engines rumbled to life. We headed south, in the opposite direction of the front lines. I was glad for that, at least.

Chapter 6

Journal Entry Four: 2 APR 2003 (2)

The road south was fairly uneventful. Well, it was uneventful for a day in Iraq, at least, and by that I mean nobody was killed or injured. While passing through some of the villages, we got fired upon a little. It was just a few potshots, but Montgomery acted like we were in the midst of some protracted firefight.

The funniest part was when we were in this little village near Ash Shabakah. We heard a shot ring out, and Montgomery ordered us to stop. Whoever was firing really sucked. I'm serious. This guy was so bad he didn't even score a hit on any of our vehicles. I wondered if he was just sticking an AK-47 out a window without even looking where he was shooting. You get a lot of cowardly bullshit like that over here. I mean, think about the innocent civilians that moron could have hit.

Anyway, so he's firing, and the lieutenant is having a shit-fit, crouched down beside his Humvee, calling for fucking air support on the radio. I could hear the colonel

THE DESERT

yelling back at him even from where I was. I couldn't make out the words, but I could tell the colonel didn't like being bothered with stupid nonsense like that.

Eventually, Montgomery orders us to move on. We left the world's crappiest sniper and moved on to the next shithole village.

While going through another village, we were swarmed by little kids begging for candy and stuff. Apparently, another unit that had come through had really gone hog wild with the candy here. I noticed no one in my truck handing any out, so I pulled out some cheap candy that I had on me. I was about to hand it over the side of the truck to a little boy when the soldier next to me, a private named Reno, put his hand on my chest and shook his head. He looked serious.

"Don't give these little fuckers anything," PV2 Reno said.

I shrugged and put away the candy. Reno sat back in his seat. He seemed really edgy.

"What's the big deal?" I asked.

"Didn't they brief you on this town?" asked Reno. "Fucking Intel weenies are supposed to know shit, right?"

"Well, I just found out about this mission last night," I said. "Could you fill me in?"

Reno shrugged and was silent.

Another soldier, PFC Rodriguez spoke up instead, "Aww come on, Reno. Cut the guy some slack."

"You wanna know, Intel puke?" asked Reno. "They're fucking devil worshipers, that's what."

"Devil worshipers?" I asked. "In Iraq?"

"Reno's overreacting," said Rodriguez. "They're called Yazidis and they aren't really devil worshipers. That's just what the Muslims call them."

"Why?" I asked.

"They practice some kind of pre-Islamic religion that pays homage to a fallen angel called *Melek Taus*," Rodriguez continued. "Christians and Muslims hear *fallen angel* and assume they're Satanic."

Reno performed the sign of the cross. "You just keep those fucking devil worshipers away from me, okay. And stop talking about them, dammit. They creep me the fuck out."

That village was the last one we saw for a long time. After that, it was open desert and the occasional lonely shepherd for miles. By nightfall, we were in the middle of fucking nowhere. The lieutenant had us find a place off the road to camp for the night.

About half of us, including myself, slept in the backs of the trucks. The rest pulled out cots and slept in the open. We got maybe four hours sleep before Montgomery had us all awake and moving again.

It was some time during the next day that we first began to suspect something was amiss. We kept stopping in the middle of nowhere and pulling off to the side of the road for a while. Montgomery would be talking into the radio, or arguing with his sergeants. He appeared to be about ready for a nervous breakdown, not a trait you really want to see in your commanding officer.

THE DESERT

Chapter 7

Journal Entry Five: 2 APR 2003 (3)

It wasn't until late that afternoon that we really began to worry. The sergeants weren't letting us know what was going on, but we knew it shouldn't take us three days to get to our objective. We couldn't understand how even Montgomery could get us lost when he had a fucking GPS locater
 That evening as we camped early before nightfall, we found out the answer to our questions. Lieutenant Montgomery called everyone together to discuss our situation.
 "It seems that our Iraqi friends are more resourceful than we had imagined," Montgomery said to the assembled soldiers. "Our radio transmissions have been jammed ever since about 0900 this morning. In addition, our global positioning equipment is also malfunctioning, possibly also jammed. I believe that they may be employing some sort of new jamming technique against us that is causing the interference.
 "However, we have been going over our maps, and we have been able to locate the

position of our target village, a place named Al Haram. We should be able to make it there by 1200 hours tomorrow. I trust that you will keep vigilant tonight, and be well rested for tomorrow. In light of the increased jamming, we may encounter a heavier enemy presence than was previously determined by our intelligence services."

Montgomery looked straight at me and gave me a look of utter contempt. Many of the other soldiers followed his gaze and correctly perceived that he was intending disrespect. I just smiled. Assholes hate it when you smile at them.

After a short pause, he began again, "Since communications are down, we have no way to call in for air support or reinforcements should we encounter heavy enemy activity. I want every one of you to mentally prepare yourselves for tomorrow. We must redeem ourselves in the eyes of our peers and rid ourselves of that stupid nickname. Understood?"

About a third of the soldiers mumbled in assent.

"Dismissed," said the lieutenant, who then turned and walked back to his Humvee.

Great, I thought. *It just keeps getting better.*

THE DESERT

Chapter 8

Journal Entry Six: 3 APR 2003

The next morning was typical Army bullshit. Why exactly, I often wonder, do we need to be up and moving at 0400 hours in the damned morning? Wouldn't a decent night's rest maybe actually make us a more efficient fighting force? I know you civilians reading this might have a hard time imagining what it's like in the field, so I'll try to paint you a picture.

    The next time you wake up in the middle of the night and look at the clock and see that it's around 3 a.m., I want you to imagine something. Imagine that instead of going back to sleep for the next few hours, you have to jump out of bed and go to work. Now also imagine that instead of those nice pajamas you're wearing, you went to bed in the same dirty old uniform you've been wearing for the past few weeks. Furthermore, that bed you just jumped out of is actually the uncomfortable bench seat in the back of a military transport truck. You have a few minutes to shave, use the latrine, and find something dreadful to eat before it is time to get moving. Oh yeah, and I almost forgot, People will be shooting at you at work today. Maybe after you've completed this little exercise, you'll appreciate more the things you take for granted.

These are exactly the kinds of things I'm thinking about at 0400 hours, as I'm getting ready for another day of fun and sun in the desert.

I am always astounded at the seemingly supernatural ability of sand to get into even the most impossible of places. This morning, I opened a plastic garbage bag that I kept some of my more important personal possessions in. Sure enough, just like every other time I'd opened the thing since arriving in the desert, the damned thing had sand in it.

I mean, you'd think that a plastic bag, twisted and tied closed, enclosed in another canvas bag, would be able to resist being inundated with particles of sand. Well, at least you'd believe that if you had never been to the desert.

So I pulled out the techno-thriller I was reading, and shook the sand out of it. I figured I had at least a good five to ten minutes of uninterrupted reading time before Lieutenant A-Hole gets the Magical Mystery Tour underway again. I was in luck: It was almost twenty minutes before he finally ordered us to move.

Now I don't know about you, but if I were in a hostile country with no working communications or navigation equipment, I might consider waiting until the sun came up before I started driving aimlessly into the desert. Perhaps that's just not the kind of thinking they teach in officer school.

THE DESERT

Chapter 9

Journal Entry Seven: 3 APR 2003 (2)

That afternoon, we encountered the village. We could see it from some distance away, not because of its size, being that it was comparably small, but rather because of the lack of any discernible landmarks in the vicinity. Miles beyond the tiny village, we could see a small ridge of hills in the distance, but they were the only other visible features in the otherwise barren wasteland.

In fact, I was kind of hoping the little village would turn out to be a mirage. I thought of how much fun I would have telling the story of *Eight Up Platoon* to my fellow spooks back in my own unit if I were able to tell them about the Lieutenant leading us to a village that turned out to be a mirage. The platoon would never recover from that one.

I wasn't too disappointed, however, when we finally rolled into the little village late that afternoon, since at least it would be better than sitting in the back of that damnable truck all day. Trust me, those are wooden benches you sit on in those trucks. You wouldn't want to spend another day back there either.

When we entered the village, I was personally suspicious that we were in the wrong town, since we had been led to believe that it would be somewhat larger than this one. However, the Lieutenant assured us that he had finally led us to Al Haram, and I was in no position at the moment to dissuade him from his notions.

THE DESERT

Chapter 10

Journal Entry Eight: 3 APR 2003 [3]

The village was remarkably compact, even by Iraqi standards. I judged that there couldn't be room for much more than about forty families in the entire town. And that was assuming full capacity. From the look of the place, I guessed we'd be lucky if it wasn't completely deserted.

As we approached the edge of town, I noticed some peculiarities about the design of the place. It was definitely not your typical Iraqi village.

The first thing that looked really out of place was the fact that this town had a city wall. Now, occasionally you will run into towns or cities in the Middle East with a city wall, but usually it is an historical relic from the past and not in use. This town, on the other hand, had a relatively new wall. In fact, it was a stark contrast to the buildings inside the wall, which appeared to be older and in a state of disrepair.

I don't know enough about engineering to be able to accurately identify the materials used in constructing the wall, but it appeared to have been built with some kind of whitish stone. It was a surprisingly uniform height of around six feet, and there appeared to be only one entrance, at least from this side of town.

The entrance consisted of a gap about twenty feet wide. The *gate* consisted of an ancient truck with metal plates affixed to one side. This way, the occupants could *drive* the gate into place.

We pulled up to within about a hundred feet of the entrance. The gate was closed. We couldn't see anyone or any activity inside the village.

I was in the rear transport truck so I couldn't hear the specific orders that Montgomery was issuing, but it looked like he was sending a squad to secure the gate. Then he gave another order, and I followed everyone else in dismounting and assuming tactical positions.

At this point in the story, I have to stop and point out that when I signed up for Intel, I had a wonderful vision in my head of espionage and intrigue. I pictured myself interrogating Al-Qaeda operatives, stopping terrorist attacks, catching spies. At no point did I think I would ever be attached to an infantry platoon in a war zone, lost in the desert, preparing to assault Mad Max's stronghold from *The Road Warrior*. I figured there really had to be a better way to finance my college education.

Anyway, back to the story. So I'm crouched down beside the transport truck, pointing my M-16 in the general direction of the village, wondering if the rifle would actually work when I fired it. I hadn't fired it since entering Iraq and I wished I'd actually had a chance to make sure it hadn't suffered any damage on the trip over.

THE DESERT

I watched as the first squad of Eight Up Platoon rushes over to the gate area and does their best to secure it. I wondered if the lieutenant had given them any specific orders as to how they would be securing the entrance, since from my vantage point, it looked like they were pretty confused. The wall was pretty solid, and the gate/truck was pretty impregnable, so I kind of enjoyed watching the infantry grunts try and figure out how to deal with the situation.

Theoretically, they could have just thrown some grenades over the side, but we had no reason to believe that people on the other side were *bad guys*. Heck, for all we knew, the townsfolk had just closed off the village so that they could be safe from the conflict outside. We couldn't just start killing people for no reason.

Finally, the squad's sergeant decided to try something brash and incredibly dangerous. He and another soldier boosted a third soldier over the wall. I sure wouldn't have wanted to be that guy. Imagine what would have happened if there were a whole bunch of lunatics with AK-47s on the other side of that wall. He wouldn't have had a chance.

Luckily for him, nobody was on the other side of the wall. A few moments later, the infantryman was able to get the truck/gate started and he began to move it out of the way. The truck looked like one of those stubby-looking German vehicles you see all over Europe. After he opened the gate, we were finally rewarded with our first unobstructed view of the interior of the village.

Chapter 11

Journal Entry Nine: 3 APR 2003 [4]

Beyond the gate was a wasteland. There were about fifty buildings in all, and about half were uninhabitable. Roofs were caved in. Walls were knocked down. There were piles of garbage and discarded building materials lying against the walls and in corners where the wind had deposited them.
 Dust-like sand covered everything, blanketing it all with the dull yellowish brown of the Iraqi desert. It didn't look like the village was inhabited at all.
 Montgomery addressed first squad's sergeant, "Sergeant Graves, the village looks deserted, but take your squad and do a quick sweep of the place just to make sure. I don't want any surprises."
 Sergeant Graves and his squad had just started to move out when I saw something that chilled me. "Lieutenant Montgomery, Sir?" I said.
 "Yes, Specialist?" the lieutenant replied with thinly veiled contempt.
 I pointed to a set of footprints in the dust leading to one of the nearby buildings

to the left. They were recent. "I don't think we're alone, Sir." I said.

The lieutenant's eyes became wider as he yelled out to Sergeant Graves, "Sergeant! We have company!" He pointed to the footprints.

Sergeant Graves turned back to the lieutenant. I can still remember seeing his expression. He was only about thirty to forty feet away from me at this time. He cocked his head to the side like a dog does when it is confused. For that reason, I doubt that the sergeant heard or comprehended the lieutenant's warning. All of this happened in a single instant. From the moment I saw the lieutenant speak to the moment Sergeant Graves's head exploded, it couldn't have been more than a second.

Gunshot wounds in real life are quite different from what you see in the movies. If this moment had occurred in a motion picture, a large amount of blood would have come spurting out of Sergeant Graves' head. Then he would have probably been thrown through the air by the force of the blast. Or if an actor of some prestige played him, he probably would have gracefully dropped to his knees before falling over dead. Maybe he could have even said something poignant before he keeled over.

In real life, death by firefight is much more visceral. It was just like his head suddenly changed shape. One moment, he was cocking it to the side like a puppy, the next it was oddly distended: a misshapen face clinging to a Kevlar helmet. There was blood, but not very much was visible at first.

But the part that affected me the most about the incident was the way that the sergeant's body suddenly became limp. It's hard to explain to someone who hasn't seen it. It's as if he were being controlled by wires, like a marionette, and then suddenly the strings are cut. He didn't drop to his knees like a warrior meeting his end with dignity. He just fell like a discarded doll, without glory or drama.

I saw all this. I heard the distinctive *pop* of the AK-47 shooting from the darkness of the doorway to my left. And yet I hesitated. This was my first real taste of war, and it was nothing like what I had expected. There was no uplifting soundtrack to motivate me to fight. There were no inspiring words urging me to usher forth *once more into the breach*. There was only the unreal sound of the firefight, which doesn't sound anything like what you would expect. I always think of it as sounding like the world's largest popcorn machine.

Before I had regained my composure enough to respond to the situation, the firefight was over. A couple of guys from first platoon were looking in the small shack where the guy who had been firing at us had met his end. One of them stepped away quickly and vomited.

That was weird to me, because I assumed that these hardcore infantry grunts would be able to take a little carnage. At least that's what I was thinking until I decided to take a look for myself. I had barely gotten near the door to the shack when the smell hit me.

"Jesus H. Christ!" I said. "Do all dead Iraqis smell like that?"

The soldier who had just vomited wiped his mouth and answered. "There's gotta be someone else dead in there," he said. "You don't get a smell like that unless someone's been rottin' for awhile."

Indeed, it smelled like a combination of roadkill and human feces. I probably would

THE DESERT

have vomited myself if I hadn't prepared myself for the shock when I saw the other soldier puke.

I peeked in from a few paces outside of the doorway. I could see the body of the Iraqi inside, but it looked odd to me. For one thing, there was barely any blood. I mean, I know that in real life, gunshot wounds are not necessarily as bloody as in the movies, but I only saw a few specks of red here and there. There were a few brown stains on his clothes that could've been old bloodstains, though.

Another odd thing was the way his skin looked. I'd never seen an Arab that was so white. He was so pale that his skin had become more grey than anything else. It didn't look natural, and it didn't look like something that could have been caused recently.

Furthermore, he wasn't wearing anything above the waist, which was something you pretty much never saw in the Middle East. He was wearing stained white pantaloons and sandals. That was it.

The weirdest thing though, was his lack of hair. His face was pretty messed up from gunshot wounds, but it looked as if he were clean-shaven. His head was shaved as well, and I couldn't see any body hair on his chest or arms. I probably would have been able to spot it pretty easily against that pale skin, too.

"Corporal Hickson!" shouted the lieutenant.

A small, wiry infantryman ran over to the officer. "Yes, Sir?"

"You have first squad for now. Take them and secure the immediate area."

"Hooahh, Sir," said Hickson. The corporal rushed away and began ordering his squad using hand signals, pointing to each man and then pointing to where he wanted each one to go.

"Hunt and Vasquez!" shouted the lieutenant.

Sergeants Hunt and Vasquez reported to the lieutenant, followed by the platoon sergeant, Sergeant First Class Patel.

"Hunt, you take your squad and go house to house. Vasquez will take third squad and cover your men. Make sure we don't have any more surprises. Understood?"

Sergeant Hunt said, "Yes, Sir."

Sergeant Vasquez just nodded. Then the two non-commissioned officers left to gather their men.

Sergeant First Class Patel stepped forward and addressed the lieutenant. "Can I have a word with you, Sir?" he said.

SFC Patel was an Army anomaly. The majority of infantry and combat soldiers are white. There is a growing minority of Hispanic soldiers in the combat ranks, but it is extremely rare to see any other minority. Patel was a Pakistani-American Hindu, generally not the normal type of guy you see in an Army uniform, much less in infantry. In fact, it was so uncommon to see a Pakistani-American in a combat platoon that often soldiers from other units assumed he was a United Nations representative. No kidding.

The position of Platoon Sergeant, the most senior non-commissioned officer in a platoon, is a fairly prestigious assignment, so it must have taken some real hard work for Patel to get there. Another odd thing about the guy was that he was just about the biggest Pakistani you'll ever see. He looked like a Hindu version of The Rock. He could probably kick the ass of any guy in the platoon.

THE DESERT

"Sure, Sergeant," said the lieutenant. "Step over here."

I couldn't make out exactly what SFC Patel was saying to Montgomery, but the gist appeared to be that he needed to lay off the barking orders. A non-commissioned officer had just gotten his head blown apart, and the men needed to know that their commanding officer was a calm, rational guy who was going to make sure no one else got killed today. Even to me, it was obvious that Montgomery was in way over his head.

When the two soldiers returned from their talk, Patel addressed the squads preparing for their sweep of the town, "Sergeant Hunt...Sergeant Vasquez...I'll be leading the sweep personally. Let's make sure no one else gets hurt today, hooaah?"

Both sergeants replied, "Hooahh, Sergeant." I could see the expressions of anxiety lessen amongst the assembled soldiers. The men obviously respected Patel, and were glad that he would be accompanying them.

All of this was fascinating to me, as my military experience up to this point had been wholly different. In many ways, the life of a military intelligence soldier is still very much like a civilian job. The danger of combat is a distant possibility, but it does not occupy your thoughts as much when you are sitting in front of a computer in an air-conditioned truck. It is easy to pretend that you are just working on an over-sized video game.

"Hey spook," SFC Patel addressed me.

"Sergeant?" I replied, confused.

"Come with me," he said. "If we run into anyone else, we'll need a translator." He grinned. "Corporal Hickson, when you are

finished checking the immediate area, find us a house for a command post and get someone to bury that Iraqi's stinking corpse."
   "Hooahh, Sergeant."

THE DESERT

Chapter 12

Journal Entry Ten: 3 APR 2003 (S)

The first few buildings we checked were empty. I even began to get my hopes up that we wouldn't be running into any more people at all. I thought maybe our first hostile had been some kind of refugee that had hidden in an abandoned town.

Unfortunately, no such luck was to be had. Sergeant Hunt's squad approached a small, dark gray, wooden structure. The color and decay of the wood reminded me of those decrepit shacks and farm buildings you always see in pastures out in the country. They'd always seemed quaint to me, but our experience in this shack left me with far less endearing memories.

Hunt's first fire team, consisting of four men with M-16 assault rifles and one man with a SAW (Squad Automatic Weapon) machine gun, surrounded the door of the building. The other fire team, identical in composition, took a flanking position to the right of the building behind a stack of wooden crates. I was with SFC Patel and Vasquez's squad to the left of the building, peering around the walls of another building we had already cleaned.

This was the basic procedure that we had used to check the other buildings so far. It may seem a little like overkill in retrospect, but I believe SFC Patel was trying to give the men a sense of safety through overwhelming numbers.

One of the men in the fire team at the door grabbed the knob and flung the door open, stepping back to the side in case anyone shot through the doorway. Another soldier was peering in at an angle, using a small mirror to see inside.

Suddenly, the soldier dropped the mirror. "We have hostiles, Sergeant!"

Sergeant Hunt, crouching immediately behind the soldier with the mirror, asked, "How many? Are they armed?"

"Two... maybe three... They're all armed, Sergeant!"

Patel addressed me, "Tell them to put down their weapons and come out slowly."

I shouted towards the doorway, telling them in Arabic to drop their weapons. I guess it must have sounded pretty weak. SFC Patel looked at me with incredulity. "Could you please sound like a goddamned soldier when you say that? Speak up, spook boy!" I repeated the command, this time with more force.

"Hell, boy," said SFC Patel. "You almost sounded like a man that time. Maybe there's hope for you yet."

There was no response from the people inside the building.

"Repeat it again," said Patel.

I shouted again in Arabic, but there was still no response.

"Sergeant Hunt!" said Patel. "Is your man sure the hostiles are alive?"

THE DESERT

The sergeant conversed quietly with his subordinate for a second. "He says he's unsure!"

"Well, tell him to use that damned mirror of his then!" Patel shook his head in disgust.

The soldier peered around the doorway again using the mirror, then dropped it and stumbled back into Sergeant Hunt, knocking him down.

"They're right the fuck there looking at me!"

Sure enough, a head popped around the corner of the doorway at a level a foot or so from the ground, only it wasn't attached to a body. A grimy hand held the head by its matted black hair. Nothing else of the person was visible.

"Hold your fire!" said SFC Patel, anticipating the anxiety that the display was incurring on his soldiers. Then he muttered to himself, "What kind of freaks are we dealing with here?"

Then, to me he said, "Tell him again to put down their weapons and come out."

Once more, I yelled the command in Arabic. This time there was a response. Three separate voices erupted in unison from the shack. They yelled with such fury that it made me jump.

The best I can remember of what they said sounded kind of like, *"Allheirux! Allheirux vakta!"*

SFC Patel jumped a little as well. Then he turned to me and said, "Well? What did that mean?"

I shrugged. "I don't know, Sergeant."

"What do you mean you don't know? What the hell are you here for if you can't even translate for these fuckers?" He was more than a little perturbed.

"Whatever they just said, Sergeant, it wasn't in Arabic. And I know enough Farsi to know it wasn't that either. I don't know what the fuck they're speaking."

SFC Patel smiled, the way people who are really pissed off can smile very broadly in the face of perceived incompetence.

"Oh great. This is just great. What are they? Indonesian?"

The Iraqis screamed again, *"Alheirux! Alheirux vakta! Alheirux viktun!"*

"Sergeant," I said. "That language sounds like nothing I've ever heard."

"Fuck this," said Patel.

The huge sergeant pulled out a CS gas grenade (That's tear gas to you civvies...) and expertly tossed it straight through the entrance of the shack. I was pretty impressed by the throw. I wondered if he had played football in high school. With his size and muscles, he should have anyway.

White smoke began to pour out of the small shack. There were no further sounds from inside. No coughing, retching, or cursing, either. We'd expect to hear something from people who'd just been gassed, but there was nothing.

Chapter 13

Journal Entry Eleven: 3 APR 2003 (6)

We waited. After about fifteen minutes, the smoke dissipated, but there were still no sights or sounds from inside the shack.
"Hunt!" said Patel. "Use the mirror and see what's going on in there."
Sergeant Hunt looked into the doorway using the mirror. He appeared to be examining the entire interior of the shack.
"What the hell's going on, Hunt?" asked Patel.
"Nothing, Sarge," said Hunt. "They aren't in there anymore."
"Fuck!" said Patel. "How'd you let that happen? I thought you had the place surrounded!"
"We do, Sarge. Nobody walked past us. There must be another way out."
"Well go in and find out!" said Patel.
Sergeant Hunt checked the interior of the shack. It was small and only one room, and there really wasn't any place to hide. He checked the walls, floor, and ceiling, but could find no sign of an egress.

"Nothing, Sarge," said Hunt. "I can't find a damned thing. They even took the severed head with them, wherever they went."

SFC Patel was so angry he was at a loss for words. There was a vein on his forehead that looked like it was about to explode. I was glad, at least, that his anger was focused on Sergeant Hunt's squad and not on me for the moment, though. Thank God for small favors.

Chapter 14

Journal Entry Twelve: 3 APR 2003 [7]

It was nightfall by the time Lieutenant Montgomery finally called off our sweep of the town. SFC Patel had kept us going over and over the town with a fine-toothed comb, but we had failed to find the creeps from the shacks or anyone else for that matter.

"We can't keep looking all night, Sergeant," said Montgomery.

"Sir," said Patel. "We know they didn't leave the village. We know they're here somewhere. They can't have just disappeared. And while they're out there, we're in danger."

"I understand, Sergeant. But we can't continue searching indefinitely. We have to make camp for the night, and I need those men here. Our mission is over, anyway. There isn't anyone here to capture or interrogate. We leave in the morning."

"Yes, Sir," said Patel.

Then, to the rest of us milling about he said, "You heard the man. Hunt, get your platoon working on securing the vehicles and setting up camp. Vasquez, your platoon can work on doling out supplies and rations. Hickson, your guys are on first watch."

Hickson took command of his squad. "I want men there, there, and there," he said, indicating peripheral shacks.

As everyone started moving towards his assigned tasks, Patel said loudly, "Nobody else dies tonight, understood?"

If only things had been so easy.

THE DESERT

Chapter 15

Journal Entry Thirteen: 3 APR 2003 (8)

At about 2200 hours, the fog rolled in. Yes, that's right. Fog. In the desert. I didn't understand it myself.
    I was still awake, finding it very hard to relax enough to even consider sleep. I was lying in the back of one of those uncomfortable transport trucks. Most of the infantrymen were used to sleeping in cots outside, or on the ground, but I had never done so.
    I saw the fog begin to roll past the open rear of the canvas-topped truck. At first I thought it was smoke. That's what it looked like, anyway. After watching it get thicker for about half an hour, I realized that I ought to just give up on the concept of sleep. I had to ask someone if they'd ever seen anything like this.
    When I jumped down out of the back of the truck, I was amazed. Visibility was reduced down to about thirty feet. I could see what looked almost like a ceiling of fog about forty feet up. The light from the moon

appeared to be illuminating the fog up there enough to make it somewhat visible.

The strangest thing about the fog though, was its color, green. I'd never seen green fog before, and this was some spooky-looking stuff. The fog was slightly luminous, and the way it seemed to shine green light on everything made me feel like I was looking at the world through night vision goggles. It was surreal.

The streets of the village were shrouded in the fog's thick soup. I could actually see it rolling in thicker all around me. I looked for the rest of the platoon and found them all awake and setting up fighting positions around the main camp.

"Jesus Christ, spook!" said Private Settipane. "What the fuck are you doing over there?"

"I was just trying to find you guys."

"Well get over here," he said. "This is some crazy shit, man."

The mysterious fog visibly unnerved most of the men. Montgomery was fiddling with his night-vision goggles. SFC Patel was giving hushed orders to the squad leaders. And all the while, the fog continued to roll in thicker.

"Sir," said Patel. "Those don't help against this shit. I've already tried."

Montgomery's fidgeting with the goggles was becoming more pronounced. He looked worried and I thought I could discern his hands shaking as he tried to adjust the NVGs to work against the fog.

"Move in and defend your positions," said Patel. "Hunt, your men take the right side and Vasquez take the left. Is Hickson back yet with first squad?"

No one answered. Patel used the radio to try to reach Hickson's men in the outlying perimeter shacks.

THE DESERT

"Corporal Hickson, do you copy?"
Static. Nothing.
"First squad, do you copy?"
Still nothing.
"Goddamnit Hickson," said Patel. "Sergeant Hunt, take your squad and bring first squad back here..."
Patel's orders were interrupted by the sound of static from his radio. The channel was open, but there was only static. Everyone was quiet, listening to the static. It was like someone was holding down the transmit button, but not saying anything through the radio.
Suddenly, I began to make out the very faint sounds of someone silently whispering. I could only hear the tiniest bits of it among the quiet hissing of static.
"...who art in Heaven...thy name..."
It was the "Our Father who art in Heaven" litany that Catholics say. He was saying it very quickly and repeating it over and over. After a few moments of this, the radio suddenly switched off and it was quiet again.
Patel broke the silence. "Sergeant Hunt?"
Sergeant Hunt looked up as if slightly dazed and said nothing.
"Sergeant Hunt? I gave you an order."
"Oh," said Hunt. "Yeah, right." He stood up. "Bennington, Rodriguez, come on guys wake up. You too, Reno."
Sergeant Hunt took his men, and they carefully picked their way towards the first shack where Corporal Hickson was supposed to be running first watch from.
Ten minutes later, they returned.
"Sergeant Patel," said Hunt. "They're gone. We couldn't find Hickson or any of first squad."

"Christ," said Patel. "Well, if they went out and got themselves lost in this fog, they're just gonna have to stay lost until morning. I can't risk getting everyone lost by going traipsing around looking for them. Right, Sir?"

"Yeah, yeah, right," said Montgomery, looking scared shitless.

THE DESERT

Chapter 16

Journal Entry Fourteen: 4 APR 2003

In the morning, there were more surprises. The fog began dissipating around 0330, finally leaving altogether just before daybreak. I'd never been happier to see the sun rise before in my life. But my revelry was to be short-lived.
　　The first problem was the fact that Hickson's squad was still missing. We searched the entire town for three hours and found no sign of them. We encountered the next problem shortly thereafter.
　　"Sir," said Patel. "They might have somehow wandered outside the village. I suggest we send a scouting party out with the Humvee to look for them."
　　"Good idea, Sergeant," said Montgomery.
　　But when the scouting party of Sergeant Hunt and Privates Bennington and Rodriguez tried to start the Humvee, it wouldn't turn over.
　　"Oh what the fuck now?" said Hunt, irritated. When he popped the hood and

looked at the engine his irritation was replaced with fear.

"Sergeant Patel? Sir? I think you better see this."

The engine was a mess. It looked like everything that could be slashed or cut had been ripped to shreds. The Humvee wasn't going anywhere.

"What the hell?" said Montgomery. "How did they get past us?"

"Hunt, check the other trucks," said Patel.

The transport trucks were similarly disabled. We were effectively marooned.

THE DESERT

Chapter 17

Journal Entry Fifteen: 4 APR 2003 (2)

"Try the radios again," said Patel.
   After twenty minutes of fiddling with a variety of radio equipment, SFC Patel concluded that we were still not going to be able to contact help. He sat down and tried to think of a new course of action.
   Meanwhile, Lieutenant Montgomery paced around the camp, his nervous appearance damaging morale. Eventually, he decided to look at the Humvee's engine again and see if it looked like it could be repaired.
   Patel stared off though the open exit to the vast and barren desert, apparently in deep thought. Finally, he seemed to have figured out what he had been thinking about.
   SFC Patel stood up and marched towards the truck that served as the movable gate for the village. He sat down in the driver's seat and cranked the engine. It took more than a few tries to get it started, but eventually he succeeded. It was a glimmer of hope in an otherwise unfortunate day.
   Patel turned off the ignition and addressed the platoon, "Okay guys. We have a

vehicle, but it's not gonna transport all of us. In fact, I don't think it's gonna make it too far in the desert anyway. This baby's seen better days. What I propose, assuming that the Lieutenant concurs, is that we send a couple men out in this truck with a radio. They could try and get outside of the range of this jamming and call for help. Sound good, Sir?"

The officer nodded. He didn't look good. He looked pallid, sickly...afraid. It was good that SFC Patel was taking the initiative and making decisions. Otherwise, I think we'd have been in even worse shit.

"Corporal Henson," said Patel, addressing two soldiers from second squad. "You and Taylor will be the team that goes out in the truck. We'll wire a commo set from one of the Humvees to a battery so that you can take it with you. Take a few days' worth of rations and water, as well as extra gas and whatever tools you can scrounge up. I don't have a whole lotta faith in that truck making it very far."

"Hooahh Sergeant," said Henson.

They began making preparations for the mission.

Chapter 18

The Desert. 22 October 2009. 1852 Hours.

Specialist Densler brought the Humvee to an abrupt halt, causing dust to cascade around the vehicle. Captain Henderson dropped the journal into his lap and gave Densler a look of intense irritation.

"Well?" said Henderson. "What the fuck was that all about?"

Densler didn't answer. He just stared ahead and to the right.

Eventually, Densler asked, "You see that, Sir?"

"See what?" asked Henderson.

"That," said Densler, pointing at a nearby hill. "See that outcropping of rocks near the top?"

"Yeah," said Henderson. "So?"

"Doesn't it look a little familiar? Like the one we climbed up about eight hours ago?"

"Fuck," whispered Henderson.

"Fuck indeed, Sir," said Densler.

"How?" said Henderson, unable to form a complete sentence.

"I don't know. I used the compass, but it led me back here. I still can't get the GPS to work."

"And the radio?"

"Be my guest, Sir."

Henderson turned up the radio and left the channel open. He was greeted with a wall of static. He left it on and just sat there trying to come up with a plan.

After a few minutes, Henderson spoke, "It's too late to keep ambling about like this. We'll make camp for the night and hope they send someone out to look for us. If they haven't found us by 0900 hours, we just head in the direction of the sun. We're bound to run into *someone*."

"Yes, Sir."

"How many MREs did we bring along on this...?"

Henderson stopped mid-sentence. A loud click had come over the radio. Densler turned the volume up. It happened again.

"Not this shit again," said Densler.

"Shhh!" said Henderson.

There was another *click*. This time it was followed by a few more muted clicks. Again, it sounded like someone running his or her fingernail across the microphone of a radio transmitter. Henderson grabbed the transmitter of the Humvee's radio.

"This is Black Two, do you read?" he said.

This clicking continued, accompanied by a scratching sound.

"This is Black Two, do you copy?"

The sounds ceased.

THE DESERT

"It must have just been some kind of interference," said Henderson.

"Yeah," said Densler. "Some kind of interference."

"Let's eat dinner and get some sleep," said Henderson. "You take the first watch and wake me up at one. Then I'll take over until morning."

"Yes, Sir."

Chapter 19

The Desert. 23 October 2009. 0155 Hours.

"Sir?" said Densler, lightly shaking his commanding officer.
"Is it one already?" said Henderson, rolling over.
"Yes, Sir."
"Okay then. Good night."
Henderson swung out of the portable cot and stood up. He stretched a bit, then went over and sat in the passenger seat of the Humvee with the door open.
Densler watched him, sleepy but unable to relax. He had this feeling that he needed to keep a good watch on Henderson. Officers almost never had to perform such menial tasks as night watch. Usually, they were the ones who got to sleep while everyone else took turns. For this reason, Densler wondered if the guy would fall asleep.
Henderson fidgeted in the seat for a few moments, not looking particularly alert. Then Densler saw him perk up.
Oh look, thought Densler. *It looks like he's about to read some more of that journal. I wonder if he'll chance turning on a light.*

THE DESERT

Henderson held the journal in his lap. In the pale moonlight, Densler could see that it was there, but the light was not sufficient to permit reading.

However, Henderson's curiosity was so great that it only took about fifteen minutes for him to justify using his flashlight.

Outstanding, Densler thought. *Not that I particularly give a shit, since being found out here would be a godsend. At this point, I'd be happy to get captured by some nutty insurgent group. At least they'd have an idea of where they were going.*

Henderson used his small, camouflage-painted flashlight with a blue lens affixed over the light to read the journal. Soldiers often used blue light at night to mimic the effect of moonlight if seen by the enemy.

He paged through the manuscript as Densler finally dozed off.

Chapter 20

Journal Entry Sixteen: 4 APR 2003 [3]

I sat and watched the old truck disappear in the distance as they drove away. I was jealous of those bastards being able to leave this accursed village. I did not like the idea of spending another night in the place.

Montgomery and Patel were arguing over how best to arrange defensive positions for the night. The lieutenant wanted to set up outside the city walls and focus on the open gate. Patel wanted to use the vehicles as defensive positions just inside the gates.

"Sir," said Patel. "If we set up outside, we have no insurance that someone can't sneak up on us from another direction in the dark. We have no idea where they're coming from."

"Sergeant," said Montgomery. "I don't like being in this shithole of a village. There are too many places for them to hide."

"Understood, Sir. But it also gives us places to hide as well. Out there, it would take all afternoon just to dig some halfway decent foxholes. In here, we can push the vehicles a little together and use them as our cover. We can retreat outside if need be."

The lieutenant sighed. "Okay, fine. But I want a retreat point worked out in advance. I don't want to get pushed up against these walls with no way out."

A soldier came jogging up to them and addressed the lieutenant. "Sir?" he said.

"What is it, McCoy?" said Montgomery.

"Sir, we've found something strange. A hole."

"A hole?" asked the lieutenant.

"Yes, Sir," said McCoy. "It was covered up, but Steadham found it."

"Take me to it," said Montgomery.

McCoy led Montgomery and Patel down towards the other side of the village. I followed at a discrete distance. They stopped at a shack that looked like every other rundown shack in town. McCoy led them inside, and I walked over to peek through the door.

The interior was about twenty by twenty. A rickety shelf ran at waist height completely around the room. It appeared to hold mostly just ceramic bowls and strange, ugly little figures of various sizes and shapes. The room smelled like road kill that had been sitting in the sun for days. In the center of the room, there was a ragged hole in the ground. Next to the hole, a dirty rug lay haphazardly, as if thrown aside. I guessed it had covered the hole until PFC Steadham had moved it.

I picked up one of the figures. I was an ugly, vaguely humanoid figure walking on all fours, but the arms and legs were too long, and the head was stretched out in the front and back. There was some writing on the base, which appeared to be in some kind of Kurdish dialect, which was kind of odd since we were pretty far from Kurd country. There was this one word that didn't make sense. It looked kind of like *lypo-may-ody* or something like that. It's hard to translate letters from languages that don't use the Latin alphabet, at least for me. I rejoined the rest of the group.

"We were suspicious when we saw the rug," said McCoy. "The rest of the shacks in this town look too poor to have rugs in them."

Upon further inspection, the hole looked larger than I had thought at first glance. A person could fit through it and maybe even carry a decent amount of gear. It appeared to cut through a layer of solid rock. It was roughly circular, and the cone shape of the entrance suggested that it had been caused by some kind of errant artillery round. It was far too old to have been created during *this* war, though. Besides, the shack didn't have any holes in the roof, so it had to have been built after the hole had been created.

Patel shined a flashlight down into it. From my vantage point, I couldn't see inside.

"Holy shit," said McCoy. "Do you think they could be hiding in there?"

"I'd bet on it, Private," said Patel. "There's a ladder leading down."

"Why don't we just drop a couple grenades in there, Sarge?" asked McCoy.

"Well," said Patel. "For one thing, we don't know if First Squad is down there being held captive. Second of all, they might have alternate exits. If we blow this one, they have to use another one that we don't know about. This way, we have the initiative. We know where they're coming from."

"I see, Sergeant," said McCoy.

THE DESERT

"McCoy," said Patel, "you stay right here and shoot anyone coming up that ladder without an American flag on his shoulder, hooahh?"

"Hooahh, Sarge," said McCoy.

"Sir," said Patel. "I think it's about time we went on the offensive."

Chapter 21

The Desert. 23 October 2009. 0331 Hours.

"What a bunch of bullshit!" said Henderson, quite loudly.

Densler jerked out of sleep and quickly scanned the area. He squinted at the Humvee, a faint blue glow still emanating from where the lieutenant held his flashlight.

"Sir?" Densler inquired.

"The journal is incomplete," said Henderson. "A whole bunch of it has been ripped out. Did you see any other pieces of paper lying around back in the cave?"

"No, Sir."

"Damn," said Henderson. "This last page is just some spooky sounding, ominous shit. Get a load of this..."

Henderson read the last page aloud. "Number one: Give up trying to leave. There's no way out; Number two: Stay up high. You are safer up here; Number three: Stay out of the fog; and Number four: Do not go into the hole."

"Fog, Sir?" asked Densler. "In Iraq?"

THE DESERT

"I shit you not, Specialist," said Henderson. "In the journal, he claims to have seen some kind of massive green fog. Sounds like chemical weapons to me."

Henderson chuckled, "It gets better, though. Let me finish. He says: *If I tell you more, you will not believe me. It is best just to leave unsaid what has happened here. It is too terrible for words. I would say, 'Good Luck' but if you are reading this, then it is too late for you. Sorry Friend, for the trap has already sprung.*"

"Well," said Densler. "We did already know he had a flair for the dramatic, what with the whole *May God have mercy on your souls* thing."

"Yeah, well," said Henderson. "I think Specialist Forbes here must have gone a little nuts as the starvation began to kick in. Without food and water, who knows what kinds of hallucinations he was experiencing."

"Sir," said Densler. "Are you aware of any kind of hallucinogenic chemical weapons that the Iraqis might have developed? Or something the Russians sold to them? I mean, that would just be the first thing I would think of to explain this."

Henderson scratched his chin. "I've never heard of it, but that doesn't mean it isn't possible. Good idea, Specialist."

As if you'd actually credit me with the idea if it turns out to be true, thought Densler. *I'm going back to sleep.*

PART TWO

The Village

Chapter 22

The Desert. 24 October 2009. 0556 Hours.

The next morning, Densler awoke to find the captain asleep in the passenger seat of the Humvee. He stood up, stretched, and walked about twenty feet from the vehicle to urinate.

It was about six in the morning: Late, by Army standards. The darkness was just beginning to dissipate in the distance, slowly being replaced by the fading dark blue of morning. Densler still wasn't very awake, but as he stood relieving himself, he began to notice something different about his surroundings.

Okay, Densler thought. *Now this is just weird. I don't see a single goddamned star in the sky. There are no clouds in the desert! What the hell is going on here? And just what is that green glow on the horizon? Chemical weapons?*

"Not fucking likely," Densler mumbled. He finished his business and walked back to the Humvee. He sneered at the sleeping officer, and then sat down against the front bumper

THE DESERT

of the vehicle. He thought briefly about shaving, and then decided that it would be better to conserve water. The sun began to rise.

Now that, Densler thought, *is one pretty damn awesome sunrise. I mean, I'm not a big fan of sunrises or anything, but this is definitely near the top of the list. Strange though, it seems as if I can look more directly at it than I would be able to normally. It's like watching a sunrise on film. It doesn't hurt my eyes. Oh well. It must be some kind of atmospheric anomaly. Maybe even the same thing that's fucking up the radios and the GPS. No big deal.*

However he tried to mask it even from himself though, Densler knew something was not quite right about the sunshine. He also knew there was something not quite right about the radios and GPS not working. And he damn well knew there was something not quite right about the fact that they couldn't seem to find their way out of this place.

Chapter 23

The Desert. 24 October 2009. 0705 Hours.

About the time that the sunlight reached the Humvee, Henderson finally awoke. Densler was standing at the front bumper of the vehicle, looking at maps that were spread out all over the hood. Henderson silently began getting his gear in order to start the day.

Well, Captain Ahab, thought Densler, *at least you had the common decency not to make up some stupid comment like, "Oh Specialist, I was just resting my eyes," or some other cop out. Not that it makes up for falling asleep while on guard duty or anything, but at least you don't take me for a fool.*

Neither man said a word as they prepared for the day. Densler checked the fluids on the vehicle, and Henderson inventoried their gear. Finally, the silence was broken when Henderson decided to try the radio.

"This is Black Two, do you read?" Henderson said into the radio transmitter. The response was only static.

"This is Black Two. Does anyone at all read me?"

THE DESERT

Henderson left the channel open, just to listen for any faint answer. He turned up the volume all the way, blaring static into the otherwise silent morning.

The static ceased, as if someone had pressed down a transmit button on the other end. However, no sound pierced the silence.

From the radio came a single, faint booming sound, like someone beating on a hollow metal object in the distance. The two men looked at each other, contemplating the peculiar sound.

Henderson lifted the transmitter to his mouth, preparing to call out again, when the second boom came. This one was about three times louder than the first. Henderson dropped the transmitter. He chuckled half-heartedly to himself and managed to squeeze out a little smile, as if saying, *"Oh silly me! Now I've done and dropped my transmitter!"*

The third boom shattered his little attempt to hide his fear. It was so loud it caused the Humvee to vibrate. Henderson nearly jumped out of his seat, and Densler jumped back from the Humvee, upon which he had been leaning.

"What in God's name?" said Henderson.

"There's no way that the volume can go that high on that radio, Sir! Turn it off! I don't know what the fuck is going on, but you need to turn it..."

BOOM!

The fourth boom shook the ground beneath them. Sand rose from the ground all around them in a cloud. Henderson defecated in his pants. Densler ran to the driver's side, reached in and turned off the radio.

In the silence, both men panted heavily, coughing occasionally from the sand in the air. Henderson's eyes were wide with fear and shame.

"Sir, it was just some kind of jamming equipment," said Densler. "I heard the Intel guys bragging about how they have these jammer trucks that can melt circuit boards from miles away. I'm sure that's all it was."

Henderson seemed to relax a little, and the shame overtook his fear. Densler reached into the rear of the vehicle and removed a roll of toilet paper, which he then tossed to Henderson.

"Jamming equipment," Densler repeated, knowing full well that even the U.S. military didn't have anything that would come close to causing the effects that they had witnessed.

Something's going on for sure, Densler thought. *It ain't jamming equipment though, or anything else I've ever heard of. I need shitpants to keep his head for now, though. I really don't want to have to add babysitting a coward to my list of things to do today.*

Chapter 24

The Desert. 24 October 2009. 0825 Hours.

Henderson spent a good deal of the morning trying to reclaim his dignity. He tossed his underwear and wiped out the inside of his BDU pants as much as he could, but in the end there was still quite a smell lingering about him. The captain even used a decent amount of his precious canteen water during the operation, though Densler was not about to try to persuade the officer against this imprudent course of action.

At precisely 0900, Densler hopped into the driver's seat, hoping the officer would get the message. Luckily, he did, and Henderson pulled up his pants and tried his best to pretend that everything was as it should be as he walked to the Humvee.

Densler smiled, watching the officer lower himself into the seat slowly, knowing how uncomfortable and humiliating it must be for Henderson. He started the vehicle and turned towards the sun, kicking up a cloud of dust.

Henderson reached over and tried to turn on the radio, but the power light wouldn't even come on. He tried it a few more times, and even banged on it twice.

"It seems to be busted, Sir," Densler said. "It must have blown something earlier." The captain nodded and sat back in his seat.

Of course, Sir, Densler thought, *it won't work. I disconnected it from the battery an hour ago. I can't have any more of that nonsense. And besides, if you shit your pants again, I'm gonna puke. Seriously.*

Ahead, the road veered to the left. Densler continued in the direction of the sun, leaving the road behind.

The Rubicon is crossed, Sir, thought Densler. *I hope we know what we're doing.*

Chapter 25

The Desert. 24 October 2009. 1202 Hours.

Three hours later, they reached another road. Densler slowed the Humvee as they approached it.

"Which way, Sir?" asked Densler.

"Come to a stop so I can take a look."

A look at what, Sir? thought Densler. *Are you going to consult the oracle? Well, I have heard of people who can tell the future by reading tea leaves in the bottom of a cup. Maybe you're gonna do some divination using the shit stains in your pants?* Regardless, he stopped the Humvee.

To Densler's enormous satisfaction, rather than dropping his pants, Henderson pulled out his binoculars and scanned the horizon in all directions. "Left," said Henderson. "Go left."

"Yes, Sir," said Densler. "Do you see something?"

"Yes, Specialist. It looks like a village. I think it's the one mentioned in this journal."

"Is it inhabited, Sir?"

"I can't tell from this distance."

Densler pulled the vehicle onto the road and turned left towards the village. After about a half mile, he could see something in the distance that he assumed to be what Henderson had seen. The shimmer from the heat made it hard to make anything out from this distance, but to Densler it looked more like ruins than an inhabited village.

As Densler drove towards the village, he glanced down at the fuel gauge and didn't like what he saw. *Great,* he thought. *I sure hope there's some gas here, because I don't think we're gonna make it back to base without refueling. This is just peachy.*

The Humvee approached the wall encircling the village, pulling to a stop just outside the entrance, which now stood open.

"Who are they trying to keep out with that little wall, anyways? Crusaders?" Densler said, and then chuckled. He looked over at Henderson, who was staring intently into the interior of the village, scanning everything in sight.

Densler reached for the gearshift, preparing to drive into the town. Henderson reached out with his left hand and gripped Densler's hand on the shifter.

"What the fu...?" snapped Densler, momentarily forgetting his military decorum.

Henderson stared straight into his face and said very calmly, "Wait. There's something you need to know before we go in there."

Chapter 26

The Desert. 24 October 2009. 1322 Hours.

"So what you're telling me, Sir, is that you think that whoever killed Eight-Up Platoon is still in there?" Densler said, after Henderson had given him a quick synopsis of the diary's contents. "Pardon me, Sir, but that was years ago."

"Don't you get it, Densler?" snapped the captain. "There's something strange going on here! The radio and GPS not working! The journal! The booming sound we heard this morning! This is no normal situation here!" Flecks of white, foamy spittle flew off of Henderson's mouth as he yelled.

Densler backed off, sensing the fear that gripped the officer. "So what do you want to do, Sir? We have to at least search for supplies. We can't go far on the fuel and water we currently have."

Henderson was staring into the village again. Very softly, and without looking away from the village, he said, "Yes. Yes, I guess we should do that. But we leave before nightfall. Understood?"

"Yes, Sir," said Densler. He shifted the vehicle into first gear and pulled forward through the gate and into the village. As soon as he passed the gate, he saw an open area to his left. What he saw there was not promising. The decrepit remains of Eight-Up Platoon's vehicles were parked there. They had the look about them that they had not been moved in many years. Densler parked the vehicle near them and shut off the engine.

Densler stepped out of the vehicle and retrieved an AR-15 rifle from behind his seat. He slowly picked his way towards the wrecked vehicles, inspecting each one in turn. He turned to look back at the captain, and was surprised to see him still sitting in the passenger's seat, watching Densler intently, but not making a move to exit the vehicle.

"Sir," said Densler. "I don't think there's anyone here. This would go a whole lot quicker though if you'd help me find some fuel."

Henderson stepped from the vehicle and drew his 9mm pistol. He walked towards the vehicles that Densler had already inspected and began checking the vehicles for fuel.

Oh yeah, thought Densler. *Great idea, college boy. I'm sure that the gas inside those tanks would not have evaporated or anything, seeing as how they're sitting out in the sun in the middle of the desert. That wasn't exactly what I was talking about, Sir.*

"I'll start checking the rest of the village," said Densler. "Maybe someone has been through here recently or stored some cans of gas in here somewhere." He moved off towards the first shack and peeked inside.

The cramped shack was empty, save for a little wooden stool knocked on its side. Sand had drifted inside and accumulated against one wall. Densler moved onto the next shack and found it much the same.

THE DESERT

There was something different about the third shack he looked into, but he couldn't quite place it immediately. The only item inside was a small wooden table against one wall. He stared at the sand below him for a second, while his mind worked out what he was seeing.

It was a few boot prints. At first, he thought they were his, until he realized that the prints were from the older issue U.S. Army boots, prior to the adoption of the distinctive straight lines pattern that every soldier wore nowadays. Furthermore, considering the fact that the door to this shack was partially open, there was no way these prints could have just stayed intact for more than a day or so.

"Sir!" called Densler. "We have company!"

Chapter 27

The Desert. 24 October 2009. 1341 Hours.

"Are you sure you didn't make them by accident?" asked Henderson, looking down at the boot prints.

Densler lifted his right leg up and showed Henderson the underside of his boot. The difference was night and day. Henderson glanced down at his own boots, and noticed they were the same as Densler's. He shuddered.

The only prints that Densler could find were those inside the shack. The wind had blown away any traces outside of the shack, but that did not give him much to go on for a timeline.

"Well, Sir," said Densler, "I don't know how long those prints have been there. But there is one thing I can tell you, and that's that they haven't been sitting there for six years."

"But that *is* a U.S. military pattern on the sole, right?"

"Yes, Sir, but an old one. And whoever is wearing them could've taken them off a corpse as well. There just isn't much evidence either way at this point."

THE DESERT

Goddamn, but you're dense, Sir, thought Densler. *You can buy those things at any Army-Navy store in the U.S. It doesn't mean shit.*

Densler walked away from the shack and continued searching the village. Henderson looked intently at the boot prints, as if in deep reflection.

"They sure are large, though," said Henderson. "They look about like size twelve or something." He continued to examine the boot prints, glancing over his shoulder at Densler.

Ok, Scooby-Doo, thought Densler, *you can put on the thoughtful Sherlock Holmes look, but I know what you're really doing. You're letting me go on alone, because you don't want to be around when I open the wrong door and run into hostiles. Does this shit normally work for you? Or have you just never been in anything close to a combat situation? Are they giving out captain's bars for correspondence courses nowadays? How the hell do cowardly shits like you become officers anyways? And just what kind of...*

Densler halted his mental rant mid sentence. He had just opened the door to one of the shacks and seen something that was just a little too familiar.

"Sir!" yelled Densler. "I found your buddy's little hole in the ground!"

Chapter 28

The Desert. 24 October 2009. 1347 Hours.

Densler didn't wait for the officer before entering the shack. He had not made a conscious decision to stop looking to the Captain for leadership or support, but he was gradually phasing out any reliance on Henderson and beginning to treat him as a liability.

Densler recognized the shack from Forbes's description in the journal. Outside, it looked like any other shack in the town. Inside, there was a single shelf running around the inner wall, holding bizarre little statuettes and clay pots. In the middle of the room was the hole. Even the discarded rug still lay to the side of the hole. From the looks of it, it had not been moved in years.

Densler walked to the edge of the hole. *Yeah, Forbes,* he thought, *you were probably right about it being caused by an artillery round. I've seen enough of them, anyway.*

The thing that got Densler's attention though, was something else mentioned in the journal. He had to look

THE DESERT

very carefully at the hole to see it in the dark, but there was a ladder leading down. It didn't start right at the top of the hole, but about five feet down.

Densler pulled out his flashlight and shined it into the hole. The ladder didn't look recent, but it was steel and did not appear to be damaged. The ladder went down about thirty feet to what appeared to be a flat rock surface. He couldn't see any farther than that. He stepped back from the edge as Henderson walked in.

"You'd better take a look at that, Sir," said Densler.

Henderson took out his own flashlight and looked down the hole. Densler walked over to the shelf and began examining the little statues and clay pots. There was something wrong about the way they looked to him. He just couldn't decide exactly what it was.

Densler picked up one statue that looked like a crudely crafted skinny dog or something. It was standing on all fours, and it had a tail, but the head didn't look like any kind of dog he'd ever seen. The head was too big, and squished from the sides. It also had a mouthful of long, thin teeth. He put it down.

The next one he picked up was even creepier. It was like the corpse of a human being undergoing rigor mortis had been stood up. The arms and legs were all stuck together in unnatural and painful looking positions, the head lolling on its side with the jaw hanging open. Yet the artist that had created the statue had made it stand up on its feet as if it could walk.

The third one he picked up looked like a combination of a bat and a buzzard. The wings and body looked like those of a bat, but the head hung low on a long neck, kind of like the way that vultures were drawn in old cartoons. The head was all wrong, though. It looked vaguely human, and there was no beak.

Jesus Christ, these Iraqi's have got some weird ideas floating around in their heads, thought Densler.

Densler continued walking along the shelf, examining the items. Next he found some clay pots. They were essentially empty, save for some black, smelly residue that seemed to be attracting flies. There were also some more, slightly different versions of the skinny dog-thing and the rigor-mortis man, and some other figures were so convoluted and strange that he couldn't even understand what they were supposed to be.

Maybe this is the Iraqi version of modern art, thought Densler. *It sure does smell like modern art in here. I wonder if Jackson Pollock's studio was so aromatic.*

At last, he came to something altogether plain in comparison. It looked like part of a tree branch. It was about two feet long and had thin, one-inch thorns here and there along its surface. The weird thing about it was the color and texture of its surface. It was a dark shiny black, without any bark or irregularities on the surface. It was as if it had been made from some kind of plastic or other man-made material. Its glossy surface looked almost greasy, and he had no intentions of touching it. Densler looked over at Henderson, who was still peering into the hole.

"Should we check it out, Sir?" asked Densler.

"What?" asked Henderson.

"Sir," said Densler, "I was asking if we should go down the ladder and see what's down there."

"See what's *down* there, Specialist?" asked Henderson. There was a note on incredulity in his voice. "You want to know what's *down* there? In the hole that Forbes said not to go down into?"

THE DESERT

"You're right, Sir," said Densler. "We should check out the rest of the village before exploring the hole. Maybe we'll find enough supplies that we can just bug out of here and leave it alone."

Once again, thought Densler. *I am goddamned astounded at this man's cowardice. Yeah sure, we'll check out the rest of the village for supplies. But I'll be damned if I'm not checking out that hole. For all we know, the bodies of the rest of Eight-Up Platoon are down there, and if so, then we need to give that information to HQ so they can be properly buried like soldiers. You know, Sir, soldiers: the kind of men who don't quake in their boots over a diary and a hole in the ground.*

Densler stormed out of the shack and resumed his search for supplies.

Chapter 29

The Desert. 24 October 2009. 1804 Hours.

It took all day for Densler to search the village. He found nothing useful in the entire town. Something that Densler felt was conspicuously absent was the lack of bodies. Even the corpse of the hostile that Forbes described in his journal was missing. He found not even a single bone, even though much of the town smelled of death.

It was now getting late, and Henderson began to pace around nervously.

"Sir?" asked Densler. "What's the plan?"

"The plan, Specialist, is that we go back to the cave and wait out the night there. I want to search it for the rest of the journal anyways. We'll figure something else out in the morning."

"With all due respect, Sir," said Densler. "I don't think we can find that cave right now. We'd run out of fuel driving around aimlessly looking for it in the dark."

THE DESERT

Damn, thought Densler. *He's getting that "crazy guy" look that you always see in the movies, like Michael Biehn in* The Abyss.

"Sir," said Densler. "I think the best option is for us to set up a defensive position near the village entrance. If anything happens, at least we can use the city wall for cover."

It sounds reasonable, doesn't it, Sir? Densler hoped. *If that idiot decides to go through with driving into the desert, we'll die out there. There's no other option. We have to wait until morning, and hope to God that there's something useful in that hole.*

"Yeah," said Henderson. "Sure."

Great. Densler thought. *Now he's not even paying attention. He looks like he's daydreaming. I believe this is the part in the movie where I say something like, "I'm getting too old for this shit!"*

Densler started off towards the Humvee to prepare the defensive position. He knew he was basically on his own from now on.

Chapter 30

The Desert. 24 October 2009. 1958 Hours.

As the sun began to set, Densler put the finishing touches on his defensive position. He used the area just inside the gate that Eight-Up Platoon had used. He parked the Humvee pointed towards the exit in case they had to get out in a hurry.

Densler had used a variety of junk salvaged from the vehicles and parts of the nearby shacks to build an approximately 3 foot high wall that ran out from the wall and partially enclosed the vehicle.
"It ain't pretty, Sir," said Densler, "but it'll do in a pinch."
Henderson didn't respond. He just walked over and sat down in the driver's seat of the Humvee.

Well, I guess you've picked your position, Sir, Densler thought. *I assume you'll be ready to retreat as soon as possible. I do hope you won't let me down.*

"Get some sleep, Specialist," said Henderson. "I'll take first watch."

THE DESERT

Peachy. Densler thought. *I will sleep like the dead, knowing that you are on duty, my fierce protector. Try not to shit yourself.*

As Densler lay on the ground next to the Humvee, the sun gradually disappeared beyond the horizon. Within a few hours, the darkness was complete.

Chapter 31

The Desert. 24 October 2009. 2309 Hours.

They were both still sitting in the Humvee when Henderson nudged Densler with his boot. The darkness was so absolute, that it took Densler a moment to understand what was happening.

"Something weird is going on," whispered Henderson. "It's too dark."

There were a few stars visible, but they seemed as if they were behind tinted glass, their luster dulled. Densler wondered briefly about this, why stars would appear so dim, as if hidden by clouds, when there was no possible way that there could be any sort of cloud cover out here in the middle of the Iraqi desert, on a night such as this.

And then one of the stars disappeared. Densler cocked his head instinctively, wondering if he had imagined it. Then it happened again. Ten minutes later, there were no more stars to see.

This is impossible, thought Densler. *What could possibly be causing this?*

THE DESERT

Some minutes later, Densler noticed that he could see the outlines of some of the shacks in the city.

This can't be right. It's only what, just after midnight? There's no way that it can be daylight already.

Densler watched, as the light grew slightly stronger. He could see where the walls of the shacks met the ground. He could not see any detail, but it was gradually getting brighter. But as it became brighter, he noticed something peculiar about the faint light. Rather than trey outlines in front of him, he saw a faint green tinge to everything.

He could see the outlines of the shacks closest to their encampment, but beyond was just a blur. He decided to try something. Densler took a deep breath and blew quietly ahead of him. He saw the faintest ripple in the air in front of his face.

It's the fog. It's the goddamned fucking fog from Forbes' journal. It's some kind of bioluminescent vapor. Why in hell would such a thing occur out here? What the hell is going on?

Green fog, just barely bright enough for human eyes to perceive it, blanketed everything around them.

Chapter 32

The Desert. 24 October 2009. 2328 Hours.

Densler looked over the defensive wall and began planning strategies in his head. This was something he did often to alleviate fear.

Okay, he thought. *If someone approaches from the front, I have a pretty good spot here to take him down. If there are multiple contacts, I fire blindly into them and jump in the Hummer with Captain shitpants. Then we drive out of here and die in the desert. Peachy. This isn't working.*

Densler made a silent inventory of his weapons. He had his rifle, the standard six thirty-round magazines, and a Marine Ka-Bar combat knife. He had often taken a ribbing for carrying the Ka-Bar, but Densler knew there was no better knife he'd rather have in a combat situation. He aimed his AR-15 into the fog and laid it on the defensive wall for support.

Densler had had a halfway decent amount of sleep so he was sharper than Henderson, who had still not rested. When nothing happened for over an hour, Densler looked back at the officer.

THE DESERT

"Get some sleep, Sir," Densler whispered, just barely audible.

Henderson looked at him for a second, considered it. After a moment, he leaned back in his seat and rested his head on his shoulder. He clutched the 9mm pistol in his hands like a talisman of protection. He fell almost instantly to sleep.

As in any combat situation, if one anticipates attack for too long without any action, one can begin to lose focus. Three hours later, Densler began to see things in the fog.

What do they call this? he thought, *Matrixing? Or something like that. You know, when your mind starts trying to make patterns where none exist. Like when you see animals in cloud formations and stuff. That's all this is. See, right there is a rhinoceros. And over there, that little bit of fog looks like Wisconsin. Nothing to it.*

That's exactly what Densler was thinking when he saw the fog ripple. If there had been any sort of breeze this night, Densler would have dismissed it, but there was no breeze. The wind was still, yet charged. It felt like being in the eye of a hurricane: quiet, calm, and still, but with a sense that at any moment, the world would erupt into chaos.

It was just a small ripple. There was a small swirl in the fog, just to the right of the furthest shack that Densler could see in the fog, about thirty feet away.

He stared at the spot where he had seen the ripple, aiming his rifle and readying to fire. He dared not take his eye off the spot and warn the Captain. He knew Henderson would wake when he started firing.

It seemed like hours that Densler sat there, aiming his rifle, with his finger ready on the trigger to fire. In reality, he only had to wait seven minutes.

Chapter 33

The Desert. 25 October 2009. 0243 Hours.

Something moved in the fog, just around the corner of the shack. Densler couldn't see it. He could only see the slight rippling effect caused in the fog by the presence of the unknown creature.

There was a quick movement around the corner of the shack, and Densler saw four or five long thin strands whip around the edge, as if something had quickly turned about. The strands glowed with the same green luminosity of the fog and seemed almost as if composed of a thin, gauzelike substance.

Densler almost fired reflexively, and then pulled his finger away from the trigger, resting it on the trigger-guard. He scanned the area around the corner of the shack for any further activity, but saw nothing else. He tried not to move anything except his eyes as he scanned the area.

A few hours later, the fog began to disappear, and by the time the first rays of the sun lighted the desert, no traces of

THE DESERT

green remained. Densler woke up Henderson around 0600, but did not tell him anything about the movement in the fog.

Chapter 34

The Desert. 25 October 2009. 0624 Hours.

Less then half an hour later, Densler prepared to move out. He had placed items that he felt might be useful, like rope and flashlights, into a rucksack. He slipped the pack on, then grabbed his rifle and walked over to the officer.

Henderson was still sitting in the driver's seat of the Humvee, staring off into the distance. He made no moves to indicate that he noticed Densler standing there.

"Sir?" said Densler. "Are you coming?"

Henderson shot Densler a confused look and then looked down at the 9mm pistol in his hands. He put the pistol in his side holster and stepped out of the vehicle.

Jesus H. Christ, thought Densler. *The guy's on autopilot. I just hope he wakes up enough that he doesn't hurt himself. I don't exactly relish the thought of carrying the sonofabitch back out of that hole.*

Densler walked down the path through the center of town, towards the shack with the hole in it. As he passed by the shack where he had seen the movement the previous

THE DESERT

night, he turned to look for any trace of anything out of the ordinary. He saw nothing different from any of the myriad of other shacks.

Henderson followed behind, picking his feet up and setting them down softly, as if he were afraid of making a sound, which seemed odd to Densler given the fact that they were walking on a sand-strewn dirt path.

When they reached the shack with the hole, Densler methodically checked the area for anything out of the ordinary and then entered the shack. Inside, everything was the same as before. Densler walked to the edge of the hole and shined a flashlight down.

"Well," he said. "I guess it's time to see what's down there."

Densler unclasped his Kevlar helmet and tossed it to the ground next to the hole. Henderson looked at him with a puzzled expression.

"You keep yours on if you like," said Densler, "but they rattle so much that I'm afraid I'll make so much noise climbing around in there."

Henderson did not respond, but took off his helmet and gently laid it next to Densler's at the edge of the hole. Densler sat down and swung his legs over the side. He slowly lowered himself in, trying to get a foothold on something. Eventually, he made it to the ladder, and began climbing down.

By the time he reached the floor about thirty feet down, Henderson had started down the ladder as well. Densler pulled out his flashlight and scanned the area.

"Well, look at that," said Densler. "I didn't expect a door."

PART THREE

The Underworld

Chapter 35

The Desert. 25 October 2009. 0801 Hours.

Densler waited for Henderson to finish his descent, examining the door at the bottom. It was a fairly sturdy-looking steel door, framed by more steel set directly into the rock surrounding it. To the left side of the door was a keypad, which had been smashed in some time ago. There was no doorknob or handle of any kind, because the place where one would expect to find such a device had been blown away. There were still black scorch marks ringing the area.

Densler pushed the door with his foot, and it swung inside with little difficulty. He shined the flashlight inside and saw a corridor stretching about twenty feet before turning abruptly to the right. He then examined the floor around the door, and noted that there were marks in the dust where the door had been opened and closed recently. In addition, there were footprints leading down the corridor.

"Peachy," Densler mumbled.

"What?" asked Henderson.

"Sorry, I didn't mean to say that out loud."

THE DESERT

Densler led the way down the corridor, pointing his rifle out in front of him, and holding the flashlight against the barrel to see where he was going. He turned the corner and continued to another door, its handle also blasted away. On this door were various Arabic symbols painted in red. The most prominent of them, Densler recognized.

"Oh look," said Densler. "Three men in a boat. Gotta love it."

"Huh?" said Henderson.

"You know," said Densler. "It's the Arabic word for 'stop.' Doesn't it look like three little guys in a canoe?"

Densler didn't wait for a response and pushed at the door with his foot. Inside was a larger chamber, about fifty feet square. There were lockers around the wall and a few tables without anything on them. Densler saw a light switch and figured he'd give it a try.

"No luck," he said when nothing happened.

"Would you quit fooling around and find what we need so we can get out of here!" Henderson whispered.

"I think we need to find a generator room, Sir," said Densler. "They had lights in here at some point, so they had to have a generator in here somewhere."

There were two exits to the room. One was a double door, the other a single door with a window. Densler went to check the single door first. Inside was an array or radio equipment, most of which was smashed.

"It looks like someone took a sledgehammer to this place," said Densler.

Henderson decided to try the radios anyways, to no effect. Densler walked back into the locker room and looked around as he waited for him. Densler opened a locker and looked inside. There was a whole outfit of mildewy clothes within, as if someone had changed out of their civilian clothes and left them inside the locker a long time ago. There were other personal belongings inside, but nothing that interested him. He checked a few other lockers and found similar items inside each one.

Henderson walked back into the locker room, and Densler took it as his cue to continue the search. He pushed open one of the double doors and beheld a short, wide corridor, ending in another set of double doors. They went through these doors as well and came into an open area surrounding by rock walls.

There was a large, industrial elevator shaft leading down. The shaft appeared to be rectangular in shape and at least thirty feet across on its wider sides. In addition, iron girders leading up suggested that the shaft had originally led upwards to the ground level.

"Well, I'll be damned," said Densler. "I guess we know why we never found any WMDs. They dug into the ground to build places like this and then covered 'em over with shitty little villages." He smiled in spite of himself.

Densler walked over to the edge of the elevator shaft and looked down. He shined the flashlight into the abyss, but it didn't pierce the darkness deep enough to see the bottom.

"I guess it's a good thing the Iraqis had the foresight to put in ladders," said Densler.

There was a succession of ladders and metal landings leading down into the darkness. It reminded Densler of the fire escapes he always saw criminals escape out of on cop shows. He didn't wait for Henderson and started to descend.

Chapter 36

The Desert. 25 October 2009, 0947 Hours.

It took about an hour to get down the shaft. Densler and Henderson had to periodically stop and relax, not so much because of exercise fatigue, but rather due to their hands and arms becoming stiff and painful from grabbing the ladder rungs. At the bottom was the elevator platform.

"I have half a mind to waste some of the fuel getting the generator running, just so we can ride this elevator back up," said Densler.

At the bottom of the shaft, there was an open area similar to the one at the top, also ending in double doors. Densler went through the right hand door and looked around. There was another short corridor ending in another set of double doors.

"You think they have enough doors down here?" said Densler.

Henderson did not answer. He just continued following Densler as he walked through the second set of doors.

Inside, they found something that they were definitely not expecting.

"A cafeteria?" said Densler. "Hot damn."

The room was fairly large, about fifty by thirty feet, and contained numerous stainless steel mess tables. At the far end was a small kitchen and storeroom.

"Sir," said Densler. "I don't know about you, but I am gonna go check to see if there's anything edible left in this place."

Densler walked to the storeroom door and opened it. Astonished, he just stood in the doorway for a moment. The storeroom held enough rations to last a small group of people through an apocalypse.

Densler grabbed a few items and stuck them in his rucksack. They were all encased in nondescript bags with Arabic writing on them, and he didn't speak Arabic, so he had no idea what any of the food items were.

Densler was just turning to leave the storeroom when he saw Henderson standing in the middle of the cafeteria, white as a sheet. He started to ask what was wrong, but Henderson held a finger up to his mouth to shush him. The Captain pointed at Densler's flashlight and signaled for him to shut it off.

When Densler's light went out, everything in the room was illuminated with a faint green glow, which was gradually becoming brighter. Henderson walked as fast as he could to the storeroom and pulled the door closed. There were no windows from the storeroom to the cafeteria, so the men just listened and waited.

After about two minutes, there was the quiet but unmistakable sound of a door creaking open. Next, there

THE DESERT

were footsteps, very faint, that sounded more like an animal than a human. The footsteps approached the storeroom door and stopped.

Densler and Henderson held their breaths, doing everything they could to not make a sound. After a moment, the footsteps retreated to the double doors, and exited towards the elevator. The two men waited for about ten minutes before speaking.

"What the hell was that?" asked Henderson.

"Not a clue, Sir," said Densler. "Ready to keep going?"

"Not really," said Henderson. "But what choice do I have?"

They exited the storeroom slowly, and found that the green fog had disappeared. Densler breathed a sigh of relief.

"What the fuck *was* that?" Henderson asked again.

"Got me, Sir," said Densler.

"Let's just get out of here as quickly as we can."

"Roger."

Chapter 37

The Desert. 25 October 2009. 1103 Hours.

Densler exited the cafeteria and walked into a long corridor cut into the rocks. Henderson followed behind, and both men walked as quietly as possible. After about a hundred feet, the corridor opened into a large, natural cave.

Densler shined the flashlight around the cave, noting the impressive stalactites and stalagmites. There was a significant amount of wires and cables running along the edge of the wall and down the corridor from which they had just come. There was water in pools around the columns and stalagmites. The air was damp and stale. Across the expanse, Densler could see a few metal shacks arranged on areas that seemed to have been cleared for that purpose. He headed toward the shacks.

Henderson followed behind. As the two men passed a large column, two arms thrust out from the shadow, holding a piece of rope like a garrote. In less than a second, Henderson was being held by dark, muscular arms, the rope firmly around his neck.

THE DESERT

Densler turned and aimed his rifle, but dropped his flashlight. It hit the ground and illuminated the area between Henderson, his attacker, and Densler.

"Let go of him!" said Densler.

Henderson tried to speak, but could not because of the rope around his neck. He clawed at the man's arms as he began to lose consciousness. The attacker did not speak.

"I said let go of him, or I'll shoot!" said Densler.

"Shoot where?" said the attacker, still in the shadow of the column. He had a point, as Densler could only see part of his arm. "I think you need to lower that weapon, soldier," the man continued.

Densler lowered his weapon slightly. He could tell from his voice that the man was American, and likely military.

The man let go of Henderson, who collapsed to the cave floor, gasping for breath. The man stepped out of the shadow, and Densler and Henderson knew exactly who he was, even before they read his name from his uniform. Specialist Forbes was correct in describing Sergeant First Class Patel as, ...*the biggest Pakistani you would ever see.*

Chapter 38

The Desert. 25 October 2009. 1123 Hours.

When Patel stepped out from the column, Densler could see that he was still wearing the remains of his desert print BDUs. The sleeves had been cut to shreds, and the pants were in even worse shape, but the name *Patel* was still visible on the left breast.

Patel's hair was still cut short, but not buzzed, and he had surprisingly little stubble on his chin for a man who had survived for six years without electricity or modern conveniences.

"I didn't know who the hell you were until you spoke," said Patel. "I guess the Army's giving out different uniforms now."

"Uh...yeah," said Densler. "Is he going to be all right?"

"That guy?" Patel asked, gesturing at Henderson. "Yeah, his neck will be sore for a while, though."

Henderson sat up, still gasping and clutching his neck. Patel scanned the man's uniform for his rank, finally noting

THE DESERT

the captain's bars located near his breastbone on the new uniform.

"Great," said Patel. "An officer that smells like he shit his pants Sand a guy who looks a little old to still be ranked E-4."

"Where's the rest of Eight-Up Platoon?" asked Densler.

"Man," said Patel sighing. "The name still sticks to us like glue. I guess we're still remembered, at least. But the answer to your question is nowhere. You're looking at the last of my unit, assuming Forbes isn't still out there somewhere."

"No," said Densler. "We found his body in a cave up in a hill."

"No shit!" said Patel. "I guess he was right about his theory, then."

"Theory?" asked Densler.

"He had this idea that the demons are unable to..."

Henderson cut him off. "Demons?"

"Well," said Patel. "We started calling them that after Forbes started naming everything down here after stuff to do with Hell. In fact, let me be the first to welcome you to Fort Acheron."

Chapter 39

The Desert. 25 October 2009, 1131 Hours.

"Acheron?" asked Henderson.

"I guess they don't teach Greek mythology much in whatever shithole college you went to, Captain," said Patel.

Henderson started to sit up straighter and looked about to yell at Patel, but he was cut off.

"Spare me, Sir," said Patel, the last word coming out with an obvious level of distaste. "I have no more respect for company grade officers after that prick Montgomery led us to this little slice of Hades. Furthermore, you smell like a coward, the kind that shits himself when confronted by the enemy."

"Would you please tell me what the fuck is going on down here?" asked Henderson.

"I don't have all day to sit here and convince you that there are things going on in this place that defy conventional logic," said Patel. "You'll see soon enough."

"You were saying something about Forbes's theory?" said Densler.

THE DESERT

"Yeah," said Patel. "Anyways, Forbes believed that the demons couldn't see anything outside of that green fog. It's like some kind of special bioluminescent light that allows them to pick up on things in our world."

"Our world?" asked Densler. "What the hell are you talking about?"

"They seem to be shifting between dimensions or something," said Patel. "Sometimes they're almost totally solid. Sometimes they are more transparent and can't interact with us. I don't know if they do it on purpose, or if it is just accidental on their part."

"And what does us finding Forbes's body in a cave have to do with that?" asked Densler.

"Two things," said Patel. "First off, you found his body. Those little fuckers always carry off the bodies of those they kill, or barring that, they get a ghoul to do it."

"Ghoul?" asked Henderson.

"I'll explain in a moment, dammit," said Patel. "Let me finish. Second of all, you said he was in a cave up in a hill. Now, as far as we can tell, the fog can't rise above about twenty-five feet above the desert floor before dissipating too much. Once it spills out of this confined area, they seem to have a lot less control over where it goes. Forbes wanted to go up a hill and see if he could stay out of their reach. I guess he did. Much good it did him, I see."

"So what are these *demons*?" asked Densler.

"Fuck if I know," said Patel. "They seem a little more dangerous than the average ghost story fare, though. Demon is a pretty good word for them, far as I know."

"And what is a...*ghoul*?" said Henderson.

"That's what happens to you when they take your body," said Patel. "They have some way of making corpses move around and do shit for them. We shot up some of them when we first got here, thinking we were just attacking Iraqi forces. They aren't good for very long, though. They can animate the bodies, but they can't slow down decomposition. After a few days, there's nothing left of the muscles to move. It's a good thing, though, considering what they use the ghouls to do."

"And what is that?" asked Henderson.

"They're trying to bring a little Hell to the rest of the earth," said Patel.

THE DESERT

Chapter 40

The Desert. 25 October 2009. 1150 Hours.

"What do you mean?" asked Densler.

"They are trying to set off more nukes down here, to blow the whole thing open," said Patel.

"More nukes?" asked Henderson.

"You know, weapons of mass destruction?" said Patel. "The whole reason we started this war?"

"But we never found any WMDs," said Densler.

"You have now," said Patel. "They're the reason for this shit. Doesn't this whole installation seem a little strange to you? I mean, a giant hole in the middle of the desert? This is where they tested the nukes underground. There's a natural chasm that goes down for over a mile not that far from here. Apparently, the Iraqis would drop their nukes down the hole and it was so deep and remote that the rest of the world never noticed."

"One day, they blew something up down there that caused these demons to be able to find a way into our world.

I guess we have Saddam Hussein to thank for that little bit of sunshine."

"He's dead," said Henderson. "Executed by his own people."

"Whoop-dee-doo," said Patel, dripping sarcasm. "I guess that makes it all worth it, then."

"So what do…did…the ghouls do for them?" asked Densler.

"They'd use them to try and figure out how to blow the other nukes. The demons don't seem to understand how to get the electricity working so that the bombs can arm. The demons are intelligent, but not by much. I stole all the fuel from the generator room a long time ago so they couldn't get it running."

"But…did you save the fuel?" asked Henderson.

"Shit yeah," said Patel. "But until now, I haven't had a working vehicle to use it in. They destroyed all of our engines the first night. What did you come in?"

"A Humvee," said Henderson. "It's parked up top."

"Did anyone else come with you?" asked Patel.

"No," said Densler. "We're alone."

"So be it," said Patel.

"Great," said Henderson. "So we can just take the fuel to the surface and get the hell out of here."

"It's not so simple," said Patel. "Haven't you noticed? Whenever you try to drive out of here, you always come back to the same spot. I'm not letting you waste my diesel until we figure out a way to make it count. I didn't survive this long just to die driving in circles in the middle of the damn desert."

"Any ideas?" asked Densler.

THE DESERT

"Just one," said Patel. "But we don't have time to talk about it now."

"Why not?" asked Henderson.

"Because you're looking a little green right now, Sir."

Chapter 41

The Desert. 25 October 2009. 1206 Hours.

"Fuck," said Densler. "What do we do?"

"Come with me," said Patel. "And shut that light off!"

Patel jogged towards the cavern wall and over to a small cave that exited the main hall. Just inside, there was a small building, only about ten feet by three feet, with two doors on each end. Even though none of the men could read the Arabic wording on the doors, they instinctively understood the purpose of the building.

"An outhouse?" whispered Henderson.

"Just get in," said Patel. "And don't make a fucking sound."

The three men crammed into the filthy outhouse. It was a single room, with four holes cut into the floor at even intervals. There were no privacy walls between the holes. The two doors had small rectangular screened windows that were about five and a half feet up.

THE DESERT

Patel crouched down on his haunches and made the universal shushing sound to Densler and Henderson. Densler followed suit, and crouched down as well. Henderson stood up on his tiptoes and tried to look through the window.

Patel shook his head and gestured at Henderson. Without the flashlight on, it was hard to make anything out in only the green glow of the fog, but Patel was clearly mouthing the word: 'No.' Henderson looked at him briefly, and then turned back to the window.

Ah, thought Densler. *This is the Captain Henderson I know and love. Give up, Sarge. This asshole will take us all to Hell before he listens to anyone else contradicting him.*

Henderson was looking out of the window, when abruptly he ducked and crouched down with Patel and Densler. The captain looked like he was about to shit himself again. Patel just stared at him with undisguised contempt. After about ten more minutes, the green glow dissipated and vanished.

"Now will you listen to me?" said Patel.

"It was human...but it wasn't..." said Henderson, his voice wavering.

"What was it, Sir?" asked Densler.

"Would you stop that 'sir' shit, Densler?" said Patel.

"Sorry, Sarge," said Densler. "It's in my programming."

"It was like a floating corpse," said Henderson. "It moved through the air, but its arms and legs and everything, well...they were stiff as boards. It was like a floating *picture* of a corpse."

"Oh," said Patel. "I call those ones shades. They don't seem to interact with us. They just kind of float around and creep the fuck out of you."

"Well then," asked Densler. "Which ones are we to worry about then?"

"Oh, you'll know," said Patel. "But it's best just to stay away from all of them. I don't know if they can communicate with each other."

"Communicate with each other?" asked Henderson. "Come on, Sergeant, do you really believe that this is anything other than just hallucinations brought on by some sort of chemical weapon? This is silly."

"So why did we hide in the damned latrine, anyways?" said Densler.

"I think they can smell people," said Patel. "At least I think the really nasty ones can. I hide near the latrine because the smell of it masks any human smell I might be giving off."

"We were in the storehouse earlier and one stopped right outside our door, then walked away," said Henderson.

"Well," said Patel. "The storehouse is pretty tightly insulated. It probably got just the faintest whiff of you and thought you'd moved on."

"Earlier," said Densler. "You said you had an idea of how to get out of this place. What was it?"

"It's just a theory, but I was just thinking..." Patel sighed and then said, "Okay, does it seem reasonable to you that the demons have actually rearranged space and time to force the ground to move under you when you try to leave?"

"Not really," said Densler. "But then none of this really makes sense."

"Stay with me here, Specialist," said Patel. "So does it seem more reasonable then that it's just an *illusion*? I mean, what if it is just thatS when you try to leave, you just *think* you are headed in the right direction, when in reality they are making you drive in circles?"

THE DESERT

"I guess that makes more sense at least," said Henderson. "But how can you remove the illusion then?"

"We don't," said Patel. "We just don't allow ourselves to be swayed by the illusion."

"And how do we do that?" asked Henderson.

"I'm thinking," said Patel, "that we strap ourselves into the vehicle with the Humvee pointed in the general direction of *out* and lock the steering wheel in place and hope for the best."

"And if we drive straight into something?" asked Densler.

"It's the fucking desert, son," said Patel. "There's not a whole lot to run into."

Chapter 42

The Desert. 25 October 2009. 1335 Hours.

"That's your plan?" said Henderson.

"You got a better one?" asked Patel. "Thought not. We don't have a whole lot of time. If those bastards notice your Humvee up there and decide to wreck it, then we're gonna be here for a long time. We can't wait. We have to move now."

"Won't it be dark soon?" asked Henderson.

"Yeah," said Patel. "Let's go."

Patel led them out of the latrine and then he began walking farther down the cave that they had taken to get to it.

"Where are we going?" asked Henderson.

"You just don't pay very good attention," said Patel. "Do you, Sir? We're going to get the diesel fuel."

"It's down this cave?" asked Henderson.

"Yeah, I hid it from the bastards. We better keep moving though, if we plan on getting to the Humvee any time in the near future."

"How far is it from here?" asked Henderson.

"About a mile," said Patel.

"A mile?" asked Henderson.

"Yes, a damn mile!" said Patel. "And it worked, didn't it? I've kept this little cache of fuel and weapons hidden from those sonsabitches for six years now, haven't I? You have any other complaints?" Henderson grew quiet.

"I was thinking, Sarge..." said Densler.

"Don't do that too much, son," said Patel. "You'll hurt yourself."

He may not look like a typical Army sergeant, thought Densler. *But on the inside, he's pure hard-ass NCO. I'll take one of him over a thousand Captain Hendersons any day.*

"Anyways," said Densler. "My grandfather had this theory about ghosts. He said that human beings have self-awareness because of their souls. As a human being comes to self-awareness, usually during early childhood, it develops will, which holds the soul together. It spreads out among the cells like a spider web.

"When the body dies, those webs no longer have the *glue* that holds them to your body and tissue. Usually, if a person believes in an afterlife of some sort, the soul unconsciously rises to the heavens, and if the person has a strong enough will to hold onto their personality, they essentially become, well...Grandpa called them *angels*... and explore the mysteries of the universe. If a person's will is less developed, he gets kind of *re-absorbed* into the collective pool, I guess you could say. Maybe even reincarnated.

"However, if a person is an atheist, or doesn't have any hope or even *expects* to go to *Hell*, well...those people don't have it so good. Let's put it this way: it doesn't take much will or effort to move about as a spirit. On the other hand, these ones don't even try. What usually happens is they are slowly pulled down by something like gravity into the earth's core.

Luckily, most of them aren't really conscious of what is going on. Some of them are, though. They literally spend eternity among the constant burning flame at the center of the earth. They can't feel anything, but it drives them insane. "

"Once you're down there, it's a hell of a time getting back out. Sometimes they do figure it out, but by the time they get back to Terra Firma, they're twisted and insane. Grampa liked to use the term *demon* for those souls, which is why I started thinking about them."

"Sometimes it isn't instantaneous, though. It's like the control is lost, but the soul takes a while to completely break free from the body. It is during these *in-between-times* that most ghosts form. The soul sits inside the body, as it slowly breaks free. He sees his own funeral, autopsy, embalming, burial... Cremation usually sets them free, but Grandpa thought it was pretty frightening, and spirits aren't as mentally stable as the living."

"Ghosts get used to the idea of living here on earth and tend to stay for a while. Heck, some end up staying for thousands of years. They learn how to interact using their own will to affect the material world. Some like to trick or scare people, while some just like to help."

"Some even become so powerful that it goes to their heads... metaphorically, of course. They call themselves *gods* and play all kinds of games with humanity. Some try to help humanity, while others are jealous of our physical existence. They make pacts and alliances, just like the living. They can't fight each other, so they make humans do it for them. So that's basically the afterlife in a nutshell, according to my gramps."

"Sounds like your grandpa was a nutcase," said Henderson.

THE DESERT

"You shut the fuck up," said Patel. "Both of you shut the fuck up. Metaphysical discussion isn't gonna help us get that fuel any faster. Suck it up and drive on."

Chapter 43

The Desert. 25 October 2009. 1523 Hours.

"We need to keep moving and get out of here as quickly as possible," said Patel.

"What's the hurry, Sarge?" said Densler. "Haven't you been down here for six years already?"

"Yeah, well," said Patel. "Let me give you two reasons. First off, as I mentioned before, we need to get up to the Humvee before it is found and disabled. Secondly, since Captain Henderson didn't listen to my instructions, there is a good possibility that they know that you guys are down here."

"How's that, Sarge?" asked Henderson.

"Well," said Patel. "You looked out of the latrine window and saw one of them."

"Come on," said Henderson. "It didn't even look at me. It was facing the other way and didn't seem to notice me or anything else for that matter. And all that is assuming that I didn't just make it up in my head, which in fact, is surely the case."

THE DESERT

"Oh," said Patel, a distinct note of sarcasm in his voice. "It didn't *look* at you, huh? With what? Its ghost-eyes? I suppose that supernatural ghost eyes work exactly the same as human eyes, huh? For that matter, does it even look using any eyes at all? We're talking about some other kind of existence, something different from your *Scooby-Doo* cartoon view of what these things are. Do you fucking understand me?"

"Yeah, sure," said Henderson.

"No," said Patel. "I don't think you do. I've survived here alone for six years. Six goddamned years. Now, you guys show up and there's just the faintest glimmer of hope that I can get out of this hell. I will not permit either of you from interfering in my escape, understood?"

"Now listen here, Sergeant," said Henderson. "I'm the ranking officer here and..."

Patel's left hand shot out and grasped Henderson by the throat. He pulled out a knife with his right hand and held it to the officer's throat.

"Let me explain something to you, Sir," said Patel. "You better listen, too, 'cause this is the only time I'm gonna say it. I'm in charge, not you. I don't give a flying fuck about your rank. The only thing that matters down here is staying alive and getting out of here, and you don't know anything about either subject."

Patel let the man go and sheathed the knife. Henderson stood rubbing his throat and coughing.

"Besides," Patel continued. "It's 2009, right?"

"Yeah," said Densler. "October."

"Shit," said Patel, a huge grin breaking out of his face. "I was set to retire last December. I ain't even *in* the Army any more!"

Chapter 44

The Desert. 25 October 2009. 1634 Hours.

About halfway to Patel's fuel stash, the cave began to get more treacherous. The easy footing of the earlier part of the cave gave way to more natural surroundings, untouched by man.

"This is where the Iraqis stopped engineering the cave," said Patel. "I think they were excavating horizontally to try and make room for more facilities down here, but as you can see, they didn't make it all that far."

The cave went from being a generally flat-bottomed, open tunnel to a narrow, twisted, natural cave complete with wet, slippery rocks and dangerous stalagmite formations.

"Great," said Densler. "It's not a job. It's an adventure."

"Why did you take the fuel all the way in here?" asked Henderson.

"The big nasties usually won't try to get in places like this," said Patel. "They've become partially material in order to interact with our world, so they can get stuck in confined places. The shades can, but they can't pick up the fuel and

THE DESERT

take it out of here. And the ghouls could go in here, but they're too clumsy to make it back out."

"Big nasties?" asked Densler.

"Well," said Patel. "I like to call them Jabberwocks. You know, like the old nonsense poem."

"What's a Jabberwock?" asked Henderson.

"In the poem," said Patel, "it was a kind of dragon creature, a boogey monster."

"And the ones down here?" asked Densler.

"Do this," said Patel. "Think of the most frightening, nasty looking creature you can think of. Then, think of that creature running screaming away from something else that was ten times worse. That's about the best way to prepare you."

"Peachy," said Densler.

"So, there's another thing I'm confused about," said Henderson.

"Go on," said Patel.

"Why don't they come out in the daylight?" asked Henderson. "If they're real, and not just illusions, then it shouldn't matter, night or day."

"It's that green fog stuff of theirs," said Patel. "They can only see things that are illuminated by the fog. In the daylight, they can't see the fog's illumination. At least, that's my theory. It's not like I can ask them."

"Another thing," said Densler. "You said they are trying to set off more nukes. How? And maybe more importantly, why?"

"I think," said Patel, "that this is a singularly important accident here. I've been thinking about this a lot. Hell, there's not much else to do down here. Anyways, maybe these demons, ghosts, whatever they are, maybe they have been looking for a way back up to the surface, and somehow the

Iraqis' nuke tests showed them a map to the surface.

"So perhaps, they want to make the trail go deeper. Think about it. We're pretty far beneath the earth as far as humans are concerned. But in the great scheme of things, we're still just scratching at the surface. There are hundreds of miles beneath us.

"What if the shades and Jabberwocks are just the outer recon scouts? What if there are far worse things beneath us, looking for a way into our world?"

"But Sarge," said Densler, "why don't they just float up through the ground? I mean, they're ghosts, right? Can't they just float through stuff?"

"Let me ask you this," said Patel. "Imagine you are alone in space, and everything around you is blackness. Which way is up? Could you find your way without any landmarks? Maybe they need these caverns as a bit of a *trail of breadcrumbs* to follow to the surface."

"But still," said Densler. "I don't get how they could be acting in such a concerted fashion. I mean, they don't sound all that bright."

"Maybe," said Patel, "they have a leader that is."

Chapter 45

The Desert. 25 October 2009. 1646 Hours.

"A leader?" asked Henderson, snickering. "Who? Satan?"

Patel shrugged. "Lucifer, Shaitan, Hades, Anubis. Many cultures and religions have believed in an Underworld lorded over by some kind of leader. If Densler's right about some ghosts going on a kind of ego trip and acting as *de facto* deities, what's to stop one of them from becoming Satan?"

"Let's just find Patel's fuel and get out of here," said Henderson. "You guys are just making shit up. There is no God, or Satan, or any of that invisible friend nonsense."

"Oh, great," said Patel, chuckling. "Sounds like Captain Coward here is an atheist. I suppose there is a nice scientific explanation for that floating corpse thing you saw earlier?"

"As a matter of fact," said Henderson, "I'm quite sure there is. Maybe the nuclear testing created some kind of other organism. Maybe we're dealing with creatures from another planet. Maybe this is all just another illusion. I mean, you said it before. You said that you believe that the reason we can't drive out of here is because of some kind of illusion, right?"

"Listen, dipshit," said Patel. "Atheism is the belief that there is nothing supernatural in the world, period. That's about the most ignorant goddamned way to look at anything, thinking you already know the answers before you even ask any questions. You're no different from a fundamentalist. Your mind's made up before you even considered the possibility that you might be wrong."

"And how is that different from you?" said Henderson.

"Me?" Patel laughed. "I *know* that I don't have the answers. But at least I'm still asking questions!"

"Sarge," said Densler. "Is *that* what we're looking for?"

Densler pointed to a wooden stake sticking out from between two rocks. There was a small white rag tied to the end of it.

"Yeah," said Patel. "I put that marker there so I wouldn't miss it. The fuel is in an alcove immediately to the right of it."

Chapter 46

The Desert. 25 October 2009, 1656 Hours.

Densler went into the alcove and pulled out two plastic five-gallon, *jerry can* style fuel containers. There were nine total in the alcove.

"Okay, guys," said Patel. "We'll each take a canister. We'll have to carry them by hand until we get to the elevator. I brought some rope so that we can hang them on our backs while we go up the ladder."

"Sheesh," said Densler. "I really wasn't thinking that far ahead. This is gonna suck."

"Indeed," said Patel. "So stop whining and get a move on. Switch hands periodically so neither arm gets too tired. We've got a lot of ground to cover, and a whole lotta climbing to do 'ere we rest, men."

The three men were much less talkative on the way back toward the main Iraqi base area. In addition to the fact that they were carrying heavy canisters of diesel fuel, they were all well aware of the fact that every step forward brought them in greater proximity to the ghosts, demons, or whatever they were.

When I get out of this place, Densler thought, *I'm done. I'm through with the Army. If they won't let me quit my enlistment, I'll just be the most drag-ass soldier in the military. Either way, I'm not coming back to the desert. No fucking way. I didn't sign on to the goddamned Ghostbusters.*

About three-fourths of the way back to the latrine, Patel stopped and turned off his flashlight. He lifted his clenched left fist in the air, the universal military sign for *freeze*. He looked back at Densler and Henderson and gestured towards the tunnel ahead.

Densler peered into the darkness, his eyes adjusting to the complete blackness of the underworld. Only it wasn't a complete blackness. Ahead, the tunnel curved slightly to the right, and just the faintest bit of green glow spilled around the corner.

Henderson looked at Patel and silently mouthed, "What the fuck do we do?" at him.

Patel whispered, "Follow me and stay quiet."

Patel crept forward, placing each foot carefully and not making a sound. Densler and Henderson followed behind him. As they approached the bend in the tunnel, Patel set down his canister next to the wall. Henderson began to set his down as well, but Patel shook his head.

"We might have to move quickly," Patel whispered. "Be ready."

Patel slowly walked forward, peering around the tunnel. He had almost disappeared around the bend when suddenly he began to walk backwards to the other two men.

THE DESERT

"Okay," said Patel. "I saw a shade up ahead. It's checking out the latrine, so I'd say it is a good bet that it's the one that spotted Henderson earlier."

"What do we do?" asked Densler.

"We do the only thing we can do. We wait," said Patel.

Chapter 47

The Desert. 25 October 2009. 1927 Hours.

"But for how long, Sergeant?" asked Henderson. "I thought we were in a hurry."

"We are," said Patel. "The problem is that right now we don't know what else is in that fog. It could just be that one shade, or there could be a whole damn dinner party full of Jabberwocks on the far side of that latrine. We can't chance it until we know."

"So how long do we wait?" asked Densler.

"Let's just see if this curious sonofabitch leaves or what," said Patel.

A few minutes later, Patel checked around the corner again.

"Well," said Patel. "I guess now's as good a time as any."

"What's happened?" asked Densler.

"I don't see the shade," said Patel, "and the fog has gotten dimmer. Usually it fades out as they depart."

THE DESERT

"Usually?" asked Henderson.

"You got a better idea?" asked Patel. "Thought not. The plan from here on out is this: we head to the elevator shaft. If something goes wrong, we go to the storeroom to wait it out. Understood?"

Both men nodded assent.

"Another thing," added Patel. "If we do run into those things I like to call Jabberwocks, you run as fast as you can until you find yourself outside of green fog, get it? Those things can't move fast but if they get you, that's it. Don't even let them get close to you, because they make this sound...it's, well, if you're too close when it does that, it will fuck you up big time."

"Peachy," said Densler.

"Come on, Specialist," said Henderson. "Stop with that 'peachy' shit."

"I'm sorry, Sir," said Densler. "Next time, I'll remember to shit my pants instead."

Patel snickered, "I'm beginning to like you, Densler."

"How will we recognize these...Jabberwocks," asked Henderson.

"Oh, you'll know," said Patel. "Besides, they're the only nasties I've seen here that walk on four legs."

Densler remembered the clay figure of the doglike creature and goose bumps broke out on his arm.

I sure hope I don't get to find out if that thing was an accurate representation, he thought.

Patel picked up his fuel canister and prepared to move out. Henderson retrieved his pistol from its holster.

"Put that away before you shoot yourself, son," said Patel. "Guns don't do much good against even the semi-solid ones. If they attack, our best way to survive is just to run fast."

Henderson didn't respond, nor did he holster his weapon. Patel shrugged and crept forward down the tunnel.

Chapter 48

The Desert. 25 October 2009, 2011 Hours.

The three men walked down the tunnel, creeping slowly and quietly. There was just barely enough green light left to see where they were going. Patel stopped at the latrine and looked around for a second. Then he turned to the other men.

"Okay," he whispered. "Let's go. Remember the plan. If the shit hits the fan, go to the storehouse."

Patel crept into the main cave, scanning around for signs of thicker green fog or ghosts. Densler and Henderson followed behind, trying to walk in the same footsteps as Patel. About halfway across the cave, Densler grabbed Patel on his upper right arm. Patel turned around.

"What is it?" Patel whispered.

Densler pointed to the far corner of the cave. There was something up there, barely visible in the faint green glow. It almost looked like the form of a man, twisted in pain, his head lowered and facing the ground.

Patel looked in the direction that Densler was pointing, then he turned to Densler.

"Go!" he whispered.

Patel ran a full speed towards the far doors, his gas can clanging hollowly against his side as moved. Densler followed just behind him. Henderson didn't run, but held his canister in his left hand and aimed his pistol at the figure and fired.

It was a perfect shot. The area where the figure had been erupted into a cloud of dust, small rock particles showering to the ground. The sound of the pistol's report echoed in the chamber. The figure had vanished.

Patel reached the door and slammed through. Densler stopped the door on its backswing and held it open.

"Sir!" said Densler. "Get over here!"

"Calm down, Specialist," said Henderson, calmly walking towards the door. "I shot it, and it's gone. You may make jokes at my expense on other matters, but I am an excellent marksman."

"It's not gone, Sir," said Densler. "Run!"

Densler pointed back in the direction of the figure. In the still settling dust, the form of a man, illuminated faintly by the green fog, floated towards the officer. It did not disturb the dust at all, and moved as if in liquid rather than air. Its head still looked down, aiming directly at the cave floor. The limbs were contorted as if in indescribable pain, fingers and toes jutting out at unnatural angles. There was no hair on the figure, nor any clothes, and the stretched-too-thin skin looked pale with dark mottled patches.

Henderson dropped the fuel can and began firing at the spectral form. Densler could delay no longer. He ran to catch up with Patel. As he crashed into the cafeteria, he saw that the room was much brighter with the green glow than the cave had been.

THE DESERT

Patel stood inside the storehouse door, frantically waving him inside. Densler ran at the door as he heard sounds coming from the direction of the elevator shaft. He stumbled into the storehouse, and Patel shut the door immediately behind him.

There was enough of the mist trapped inside the storehouse for Densler to see Patel. He stood against the door, holding a finger up to his mouth in a signal that Densler should be quiet.

Densler could hear the double doors of the elevator side entrance to the cafeteria burst open. He could hear something big and heavy moving about in the cafeteria, then it exited the room through the door that he and Patel had come through only seconds before, the sounds of its feet dying in the distance.

There followed about a minute of absolute silence. Densler was about to ask Patel what they should do about Henderson, when the silence was broken by the sound of gunshots in the distance, deep in the cave. Patel shook his head.

A sound erupted from outside, in the direction of the cave. It was a combination of two distinct sounds. The first was the deep bass of a foghorn, so low in frequency that it was almost inaudible to the human ear, yet at the same time so powerful that it caused pain, even at this distance. The accompanying sound was at the other end of the spectrum, a high-pitched, piercing tone that made Densler's head spin.

Densler fought to control the sudden urge to vomit. Patel winced, and tried not to show that he was also feeling the effects of the sound.

Patel turned to Densler and mouthed a single word: "Jabberwock."

PART FOUR

The Slave

Chapter 49

The Desert. 25 October 2009. 2021 Hours.

There were no further gunshots, and to both men's great relief, the Jabberwock also remained silent. Patel and Densler were still for another ten minutes before either chanced to speak.

"Henderson?" whispered Densler.

"They only make that sound when they are pursuing someone," said Patel. "Since they move so slow, they make that howl to slow down their prey. Think about how it felt. We're a couple walls and about a hundred feet away from where that thing was, and it made me want to pass out. Imagine how it was for Henderson in the same room with it. He's gone. No doubt about it."

"The first time we came upon one, it made Sergeant Hunt's ears bleed. We fired hundreds of rounds into the thing. Little shreds of flesh would come off, but it didn't slow it down. The little pieces of skin would float, like the damn thing was in water, and eventually they'd fade away."

THE DESERT

"Hunt was so pissed off at the thing that he grabbed an AT-4 rocket launcher from Rodriguez and fired it straight at the thing. It went in one side and came out the other, didn't even detonate. Left a nice clean hole in its ribcage, though. Didn't do any good. It didn't even seem to notice."

"Their only weakness is their slow speed. I think maybe it has to do with their being kind of in both worlds. If you watch them walk, it's like they're bogged down in mud or something. Not that it matters, since they just howl at you and you're fucked."

"We'll camp here for the night," said Patel. "No point going out now."

"We're not going to try for the Humvee?" asked Densler. "Won't they destroy it?"

"Son," said Patel. "That Jabberwock was coming from the elevator shaft. It only goes to one place. He was coming back from the village. We're already too late."

Chapter 50

The Desert. 25 October 2009. 2020 Hours.

"So what's the plan, then?" asked Densler.

Patel chuckled. "The plan then, is that we sit here for a day or so and wait for the frenzied bastards to calm down. Trust me, once one of them finds a kill, the rest of them run around crazy for hours, sometimes even days. It's like when a shark makes a kill, and every other shark in five miles shows up because they smell blood. We're not going anywhere for a while."

"I guess it's a good thing we're in the storehouse then," said Densler.

"Trust me," said Patel. "I've been eating these Iraqi rations for six years now. You'll be begging for death soon enough." He smiled.

"Well," said Densler. "I'm so damned hungry that I don't care at this point."

Densler stood up slowly, trying not to make too much sound. He walked among the aisles of white boxes that held the dried Iraqi rations.

THE DESERT

"Densler," said Patel. "I've got some survival gear stowed in here as well. This isn't the first time I've hid here. On the shelf to your right, you'll find blankets, candles, matches, and stale water. Take what you need."

An hour later, Densler and Patel sat across from each other at the rear of the storeroom. Each man had sat up with a blanket wrapped around him.

"Jesus Christ, Sarge," said Densler. "You weren't kidding about these rations. I mean, it looks like cereal, but it tastes like paper."

"It'll keep you alive, at least," said Patel.

"So," said Densler, after choking down his latest spoonful of chalky goodness, "have they ever tried to get in here? I mean, how safe are we?" "A Jabberwock tried once," said Patel. "but not seriously. It just pushed against the door a bit before moving on. I expect that if it wanted to, one of them could probably get in."

"And the uh, shades?" asked Densler. "Can't they move through walls?"

"They can," said Patel. "But they've never come in here when I've been hiding. Maybe they've checked it out a few times, and don't think it's worth looking at again. Don't forget that we don't know how intelligent or non-intelligent they are. The shades are especially hard to pin down because they don't seem to do much of anything. You can't make a generalization based on that little evidence. It's best just to be wary of them all."

"Can't argue with that, Sarge," said Densler.

Patel jerked his head up and went quiet.

"What is it?" asked Densler.

"Shhh!" said Patel.

Densler listened, but could hear nothing in the absolute stillness of the underground base. After about two minutes, he heard a muffled thump from far away.

"It's them," whispered Patel. "The Jabberwocks. They're pouring into the main cave chamber."

"How can you hear that?" asked Densler.

"Your ears adjust after six years," said Patel. "And if we don't come up with another way out of here, then your ears are going to adjust as well. Get it?"

"Peachy," said Densler.

THE DESERT

Chapter 51

The Desert. 26 October 2009. 0430 Hours.

Eight hours later, the sounds coming from the main chamber faded away. The green glow had long since disappeared from inside of the storehouse, and Densler held watch by candlelight as Patel slept.

Finally, thought Densler. I *thought those bastards were gonna poke around in there forever. I wonder how long Patel is gonna want to stay in this place before he decides that the coast is officially clear?*

A sound boomed from the main chamber. It was still muffled, but it was much louder and more mechanical in nature than the previous noises.

And then something very unexpected occurred. For a brief moment, Densler didn't even realize what was happening. After being in an underground cave for almost two whole days, his eyes had trouble focusing as overhead fluorescent lights flickered and came to life.

"Sarge!" shouted Densler, momentarily forgetting that he should be whispering.

"What the hell?" said Patel, scrambling to his feet. "This is not good."

"I thought you said they couldn't do that, Sarge," said Densler.

"Yeah, well," said Patel. "I'll bet they grabbed the fuel cans from Henderson. I kept those demons from touching that fuel for six years, and then all it takes is one goddamned officer to screw it up."

"But how did they get the generator working?" said Densler. "I mean, didn't you say they didn't have the ability to do that?"

"Well," said Patel. "There is one way that they might have done it, but I really don't want to discuss that possibility right now. The important thing is that they *did* do it, and now we have to deal with the ramifications."

"Ramifications?" asked Densler.

"Yeah," said Patel. "Ramifications. Having the generator on makes the lights come on all over the place. That makes it very hard for them to see. If they turned on the power, then there's only one reason they did so. They've found a way to set off the nukes."

THE DESERT

Chapter 52

The Desert. 26 October 2009. 0502 Hours.

"We better get out of here, Sarge," said Densler.

"Now why would I want to do a thing like that?" asked Patel.

Densler found himself in the strangest of predicaments. He was uncharacteristically speechless.

"I know what you're thinking," said Patel, "but before we even try to leave, we have to stop the bastards from setting off those nukes. Look at the shit that has been created here. Imagine what could happen if they succeed, and more of those bastards come out. Sure, right now it's just a shithole village in the middle of a desert, but imagine what would happen if they begin spreading to other areas. We have to stop them."

"Stop them?" said Densler. "How? I saw what happened when Henderson shot at that ghost with a pistol. Nothing."

"You're missing something," said Patel, "and I hope it won't come as too much of a shock to you when you figure it out. Now let's get going while they haven't figured out how to shut off the lights."

"Will they be able to see us with all the lights on?" asked Densler.

"Depends on how bright each room is," said Patel. "Stay as close to the lights as possible because they are definitely going to be hanging around when we go down there."

Patel and Densler gathered their equipment and prepared to leave.

"Leave the fuel here in the storeroom. I still want to take it upstairs after we deal with the generator."

"Why bother?" asked Densler. "You said the Humvee would have been wrecked by now."

"Nothing is certain, my friend," said Patel. "Besides, I have a Plan B that might actually come in handy now. I have never thought of risking it before, but after this engagement, I have a feeling our hosts are going to make it very unpleasant for us around here."

"You have any other weapons on you?" asked Patel.

"I just have this AR-15," said Densler, "but I might as well leave it here."

"No," said Patel. "You take it along with us. We might just need it after all."

"And you?" asked Densler. "What are you carrying?"

"Just a knife," said Patel, "but it'll do."

Chapter 53

The Desert. 26 October 2009. 0509 Hours.

As the two men exited the storeroom, Densler saw the cafeteria in full light for the first time.

"Shit," said Densler. "You get used to the way things look in the green fog. You can't see detail so well, like when you are looking through night-vision goggles."

In the harsh white of the fluorescent lights, Densler saw the advanced state of decay that had descended upon the room. Dirt and dust covered most surfaces. There were black splotches where blood had dried years ago, and even the remains of trails and spatter upon the wall.

"Was there a battle in here or something?" asked Densler.

"You could call it that," said Patel. "I had forgotten, or tried to forget, most of what happened in here. It was a long time ago, but in here...it seems like it just happened."

Patel walked across the room toward the doors leading to the main chamber.

"Let's just get this over with," said Patel.

They walked toward the main chamber, and stopped at the doors leading out into it. Patel took a deep breath.

"It's not going to be as bright in there," said Patel. "We need to watch the shadows. If you see anything green, stay out of it. Make no mistake, the next room is going to be absolutely crawling with nasties, whether we can see them or not. Luckily for us, they won't see us either, as long as we stay in the light, okay?"

"Roger," said Densler. "So what's the plan?"

"The first thing we need to do," said Patel, "is get to the large metal shed at the edge of the big hole. We have to shut down any kind of equipment that might be turned on in there."

"Why don't we just cut the power and leave?" asked Densler.

"Since we're here, we oughtta make sure this can't happen again," said Patel. "First we destroy the electronics controlling the nukes. If we cut the power first, we won't be able to do anything before we leave. I am gonna set an incendiary grenade on the generator, which will give us less than a minute to get out of here before the lights go out."

"Anything else?" asked Densler.

"Let me go into the shed first," said Patel. "I don't think you are going to want to do what needs to be done in there. I've already done it before, so I won't hesitate."

"What do you mean, Sarge?" asked Densler.

"Damn, but you're dense," said Patel. "You haven't figured it out yet? Who do you think's running the controls in there, a fucking ghost? It's your friend, Henderson."

THE DESERT

Chapter 54

The Desert. 26 October 2009. 0520 Hours.

"But Henderson's dead," said Densler.

"I told you before," said Patel. "They can reanimate the dead for a short while. Henderson's long gone, but they can make his body do things for them. Let's go."

Patel slipped through the door and ran to a spot directly beneath a large floodlight pointing down from the ceiling. He gestured for Densler to follow, and he did. They moved like this, running from spotlight to spotlight, until they were just outside of what Patel had referred to as the *big hole*.

Densler saw how much of an understatement that had been. There was an enormous crack in the earth, about twenty feet wide at its widest point. It stretched to the right into a smaller cave, and to the left, it stopped right about at the cave wall. Floodlights illuminated it from all angles, and there were smaller lights running down a cable into the depths of the chasm. Cables, wires, and chains stretched down into the abyss until they appeared to disappear, deep in the bowels of the earth. The cables and wires all came from one place, a metal building to their left.

Patel nodded his head in the direction of the metal building and then crept slowly toward it. Densler followed after. He could see that the door, a rusty piece of flimsy metal, hung ajar and appeared to be clinging to the building only by the lower hinge. Up close like this, Densler saw that the shed was severely rusting on the outside and that the building was poorly constructed, little more than a shack.

The worst part, though, was the smell. Densler had smelled it before, when on a patrol a few years ago he had come across a dead sniper in a building. He was checking out some abandoned buildings and found some poor bastard that had died while waiting for someone to kill. The man had been older, probably in his late sixties or early seventies, and from the looks of things, he had died of a heart attack while sitting in the upper window of the building.

Densler had often wondered about the man's final thoughts as he lay dying. Did the irony of his situation force him to confront his deeds, or did he just cling to an unexamined life with the primal urgency of instinct?

Regardless, the corpse had stunk, and badly. Densler remembered thinking that it was not anything like what he had expected.

Nobody ever likes to admit that the smell of a corpse is often reminiscent of fecal matter, thought Densler. *Our view of death is somewhat romanticized to the point that we like to pretend that even our corpses are immune from such distasteful issues. Maybe that's part of the whole appeal of embalming; washing away that stink so no one knows it was there.*

Densler shrugged off the thoughts of death and turned his thoughts to the metal building ahead.

So this is what constituted the Iraqi nuclear program, thought Densler. *I don't even wanna know what their space program would have looked like. I'm surprised the generator*

THE DESERT

actually requires fuel. I mean, shouldn't it be, like two camels and a donkey powering this fiasco?

Patel reached the door and peeked into the gap caused by the door hanging ajar. He stepped back and straightened up. Next, he removed a large hunting knife from a sheath attached to his belt. He looked over at Densler and shook his head. He mouthed silently, "Stay here," to Densler.

Patel threw open the door and ran inside. Densler could hear a scuffle ensuing inside. Then he heard a gunshot.

"Fuck this," said Densler.

He ran into the metal shed and saw Patel struggling with Henderson; only it didn't look much like Henderson anymore.

Chapter 55

The Desert. 26 October 2009. 0529 Hours.

Densler froze just inside the doorway of the building. There were two long tables, one on each wall to his left and right, and folding metal chairs pushed up to them. Computers and large pieces of electronic equipment covered the tables. At the far end of the room, Patel struggled with the corpse of Captain Henderson.

Patel's left hand grasped Henderson's right wrist, and Densler could see that the corpse was holding a pistol in that hand. The handle of Patel's knife stuck out of the middle of Henderson's chest, where it had been buried to the hilt. Henderson's left hand grasped Patel around the neck, and Patel was fighting with his free hand to get it off.

Normally, Densler was the kind of soldier who would not have hesitated to defend a fellow soldier. In this case, it was not so much even that he hesitated, per se. Rather, he was shocked by the appearance of Henderson so much that he lost a few seconds trying to make sense of what he was seeing.

THE DESERT

The corpse still wore Henderson's uniform, but it had become bloated in the legs and midsection, causing the pants to become taut. There were black stains covering much of the lower half of the uniform. Henderson's skin had become a dark, almost black shade, and Densler would not have recognized the corpse as belonging to Henderson had he not been expecting it. The eyes were milky and faded, and the eyelids had swelled almost shut. The corpse's head lolled back on its neck as if the creature didn't seem to care about it. As it and Patel struggled, the head bounced around, making it almost look like Patel was just fighting a lifeless dead body.

After a few seconds, Densler recovered and ran towards the melee. He tried to wrestle the gun away from the corpse's hands, but the creature gripped the pistol like a vise. Patel was still struggling, but his face was losing color, and Densler saw that he had to do something.

Densler lifted his rifle and placed it point blank against the corpse's head. He fired, causing the head to explode, though not in the manner usually depicted in Hollywood movies. The face split into two large pieces, with much of the face lying on the corpse's shoulders and pretty much everything else falling to the ground behind them.

The corpse didn't seem to notice. There was not even a momentary reprieve or rest for Patel, who still looked as if he were about to choke to death. Densler placed the rifle's muzzle against the shoulder where the left arm began and fired again.

The arm was still attached to the corpse by a small amount of muscle and skin, but it was enough to cause it to loosen its grip on Patel's throat. Patel and Densler pried the hand off, and Patel grabbed the pistol with his right hand.

"Do it to the other one," Patel growled, his voice ragged from the choking.

Densler obliged, firing into the corpse's other shoulder, this time completely severing the arm. Patel kicked the corpse onto the ground where it writhed and tried to right itself. He sat down on its chest and retrieved the knife sticking out of the corpse's non-functioning heart. Patel then stood up and grabbed one of the corpse's booted feet.

"Grab the other one," he croaked, still in obviously pain from the ghoul's attack.

The two men dragged the corpse, kicking and wiggling, out of the room and over to the edge of the chasm. Patel kicked at it until it fell over the side. They watched it fall until it became so tiny they could not even see it anymore. There was no sound of the body hitting a final resting place.

I guess I know now why we never found any bodies, thought Densler. *That's a pretty effective cemetery you've found, Sarge.*

"Let's go," said Patel. "I still want to destroy the equipment before we cut off the power."

Patel and Densler reentered the metal building and they began ripping out wires and knocking equipment to the ground. Patel picked up one of the metal chairs and used it to smash in the computer monitors.

"Where are the nukes, then?" asked Densler.

"It looks like they were lowered into the big hole using the chains hanging down into it," said Patel. "They did that years ago. As far as I'm concerned, they can stay down there. They won't do the demons any good without some way of detonating them."

"Are you doing okay, Sarge," asked Densler.

THE DESERT

"Yeah," said Patel. "Hell, my throat's a little scratchy, that's all. Suck it up and drive on. Are you ready for the next part?"

"Not really," said Densler.

"Of course not," said Patel, smiling. "We're about to bring the entire weight of Hell crashing down upon us. Most likely, we'll never even make it to the elevator shaft. But at least they won't be able to use our bodies to blow the nukes. Short of them happening upon some kind of demonic engineering team, I believe that little plan of theirs has been shot all to, well...Hell."

Chapter 56

The Desert. 26 October 2009. 0556 Hours.

"Where's the generator room?" asked Densler.

"Over there," said Patel, indicating another metal building about thirty feet away.

"Are you sure we'll be able to get out of this chamber before the power goes out?" asked Densler. "It's pretty far away from the exit, and there's an awful lot of crap in our way."

Patel shrugged. "What choice do we have?"

"Well, for starters," said Densler, "we destroyed the command center for the nukes. They can't detonate them anymore. Why take out the power now? Doesn't that just make it harder for us to escape?"

"Normally, I'd agree with you. The problem is, Henderson already initiated a countdown on the nukes before I got to him. We've got about ten minutes to shut the power down before nine nuclear warheads simultaneously detonate at the bottom of that hole."

"No pressure or anything," said Densler.

"Change in plans, though," said Patel. "There's no point in you waiting for me to set these grenades. You run ahead and get the fuel. Start going up the ladders and I'll catch up to you."

"No way, Sarge," said Densler. "I'm not leaving you alone."

"Just do it," said Patel. "Anything else would just be stupid. Besides, I've escaped from these demonic sonsabitches for six years, and today's not the day that I'm gonna let them get me, understood?"

Patel turned and walked into the generator room. Densler lingered and watched him go.

"Get the hell out of here, son," said Patel. "I can't delay too long before setting these grenades."

Densler ran out of the room, down the corridor, and into the cafeteria. He flung open the storeroom door and grabbed the two fuel cans and set them outside. He used rope to tie them together, with about two feet of slack between them, and then carried them out of the cafeteria toward the elevator shaft.

At the base of the shaft, Densler took off his backpack, and tied the rope connecting the canisters to the back of his web-gear straps so they would hang off of his back as he ascended the ladder. They were very heavy, but at least the web-gear distributed some of the weight off of any single point on his back.

He looked up into the shaft, and the ladder stretched away for what seemed like forever. With the lights on, the shaft seemed like an insurmountable tower with no end in sight. His heart sank, but he knew he had no other option. Densler began ascending the ladder, slowly at first, then gaining confidence and speed. About fifteen feet up, he began to think that it wouldn't be so bad, as long as he could keep this pace going.

And then the power went out.

PART FIVE:

The Ascent

Chapter 57

The Desert. 26 October 2009. 0611 Hours.

It took Densler a moment for his eyes to adjust, and when they did, he didn't like what he saw. The entire elevator shaft was bathed in the green glow of the fog. Now that he had thought of the comparison to how the world looks in night-vision goggles, he believed that it was a pretty good way to describe it.

He scrambled up the ladder, momentarily letting himself panic, before he stopped. He clung to the ladder, forty feet up, and panted.

Shit, Densler, he thought. *You better get a hold of yourself right now. Panicking is for assholes like Henderson. It's time to calm down and climb this ladder, then go home and have a beer, got it?*

He began climbing again, this time getting into a rhythm. At about this exact moment, Patel crashed through the doors into the elevator shaft. He ran up to the ladder and began frantically climbing up. Unencumbered like Densler, he caught up to him almost immediately.

THE DESERT

"Let me take one of those canisters," said Patel.

"Uh, Sarge," said Densler, "I didn't really plan for that. They're tied to my web-gear. I didn't bring any more rope."

"Just take off your web-gear then," said Patel, "and I'll carry both of them. I'm stronger than you anyways."

Patel looked down and then said, "Fuck! No time! Climb!"

Densler looked down the ladder. Forty feet below them, a spectral creature stood at the bottom of the ladder. Its body was almost translucent, appearing frail and ghostly. It had four legs, the two in front being slightly shorter than the rear. Its appendages were thin and wiry, the muscles and sinew plainly visible beneath its transparent skin. It had a tail that appeared to be only approximately one and a half inches in diameter at its thickest point. The torso was also thin, with a frail ribcage enclosing visible organs within. Wispy translucent ribbons of dead skin hung from the beast as if it wore tattered clothing. The shreds of skin floated around the creature, seemingly unaffected by gravity.

Its head, which had turned to face upward at Densler and Patel, was shaped like a large, elongated human head. Although only ten inches wide, the head looked like it had been stretched at the top and bottom and was nearly two feet tall. The eye sockets were nothing but dark recesses that contained a tiny pinpoint of green light. The gaping maw of the creature was filled with long, clear teeth, many of which were almost an inch and a half long.

Densler scrambled up the ladder, moving so fast he almost slipped. Patel followed right behind.

Densler kept thinking of the same word, repeating it over and over in his head: *Jabberwock*.

Chapter 58

The Desert. 26 October 2009. 0623 Hours.

At about a hundred feet from the floor of the shaft, Densler and Patel reached the first landing. It was here that Densler began to really doubt the wisdom of attaching the cans to the web-gear on his back.

While climbing the ladder, the cans hung down below his waist. This wasn't a problem because they were dangling over an empty space, and the weight of the cans was dispersed through his back via the web-gear.

However, the opening leading into the landing was not made for someone with hanging five-gallon gas cans. It was very tricky to get through the landing opening without getting caught up. Once he finally made it through, he collapsed onto the landing to rest a moment. Patel practically shot through the opening as soon as Densler was through.

"Come on, soldier," said Patel. "We have to go, now!"

Densler leaned out of the landing to look down. The first Jabberwock had begun to climb up the side of the rock face. Its feet seemed to disappear about an inch into the

THE DESERT

rock face as it climbed. It slowly picked its way upward, only lifting one foot at a time, reminding Densler of a spider. It was about fifty feet up, halfway to them.

Behind it were two more, each slightly different. One of them had wispy black hair on its head that moved around as if underwater. The third one moved faster than the previous ones and appeared that it might overtake them. It shook as if shivering from the cold, and chattered its sharp, transparent teeth together. Yet, there was no sense of apparent weakness, and to Densler, the chattering seemed more malevolent than pitiful, as if the creature were laughing or maybe just impetuous.

Regardless, the sight of the ghastly trio was more than enough to spark him into action. He stood up and turned to climb the ladder.

"Let me take the fuel cans," said Patel. "Take off your web-gear."

"No time!" said Densler. "Maybe on another landing."

Before Patel could protest, Densler scurried as fast as he could up the ladder. Densler was already computing the speed of the Jabberwocks' climbing in his head and comparing it with how fast he was ascending the ladder. He figured that right now they were pretty much traveling at the same speed, but he and Patel had a decent lead. If nothing happened, and they didn't slow down, then maybe they had a chance.

And then something happened.

Chapter 59

The Desert. 26 October 2009. 0706 Hours.

As Densler climbed towards the next landing, he saw something move out of the corner of his right eye. He turned his head and beheld the figure of a teenage girl, her body contorted with rage, silently floating next to him. Her skin, or the illusion of her skin, appeared to have shrunk, leaving her lips pulled back, and her eye sockets gaping, white orbs without pupils inside. Densler slipped and almost fell.

"Densler!" said Patel. "It's just a shade. It can't hurt you! Ignore it!"

The ghost of the teenage girl floated down the shaft, apparently oblivious to everything around it. Densler turned back to the ladder and began climbing again, furiously attempting to make up for the precious seconds wasted by his encounter with the shade. He reached the second landing, and quickly shrugged off the web-gear while Patel climbed up.

"Go ahead," said Patel. "I'll be right behind you."

"Sarge," said Densler. "Come on! Cut this hero shit!"

THE DESERT

"It's not me trying to be a hero," said Patel. "If I don't make it up there with these cans, then you're gonna die too! We'll just move faster if you're in front. Now, go!"

Densler started climbing the next section of ladder. He turned back as Patel followed.

"How many of these landings are there, anyways?" asked Densler.

"Forty-eight!" replied Patel.

"Jesus," whispered Densler.

When Densler reached the third landing, he turned to look at the progress of the Jabberwocks. To his relief, it appeared that they were farther behind than they had been the last time he had looked, though the chattering one had indeed moved into the lead position. And then all Hell broke loose.

The rear Jabberwock, the one with the hair, stopped climbing, opened its mouth, and howled, making the horrible combined sound of low bass and high pitched wail. Although there was a gap of almost seventy feet from the creature to Densler, the sound caused him to vomit over the side of the landing. He had to grab the railing to keep from falling down, as he also became quite dizzy.

Patel climbed up onto the landing and grabbed onto the rail for support. He was panting heavily, and a drop of blood ran down his face from his nose.

"I...fucking...hate...those...bastards..." he wheezed.

"Do you need me to take the fuel cans back?" asked Densler.

"What?" asked Patel. "No. It'll take more than that crap to do me in." He stood up. "Well, get going!"

Densler began to climb the next ladder, and Patel followed behind.

Chapter 60

The Desert. 26 October 2009. 0759 Hours.

Just before the twenty-second landing from the ground, the Jabberwock howled again. This time, the men were a little more prepared, and farther away.

"Goddamnit," said Densler. "That shit is getting really old, real fast. I feel like my guts are vibrating."

"They do it to slow down their prey," said Patel. "I really shouldn't have to tell you this, but stop slowing down when they do it!"

"But Sarge," said Densler. "I'm so nauseous that I feel like I'm gonna puke again."

"Let me tell you something," said Patel. "First off, you aren't gonna puke again, 'cause there's nothing left to puke up. Secondly, if one of those things gets you, nausea will be the last of your worries. Hoo-aah?"

"Hoo-ahh," replied Densler, with very little feeling.

Densler climbed onto the landing and checked on theprogress of the Jabberwocks. They were about ninety feet below them now. He smiled.

THE DESERT

"Don't get cocky," said Patel. "Get moving. At this rate, we don't stand a chance."

"What do you mean?" asked Densler. "We're losing them."

"Yeah," said Patel. "But we're not losing them by enough. What do you think is going to happen when we get topside, eh? We've got to get out of the village as soon as possible."

"But it will be daylight by the time we get there," said Densler.

"Maybe," said Patel. "Maybe not. You're guessing. Besides, we have a lot of shit to get prepared before we can leave, assuming these bastards aren't stupid enough to have left your Humvee untouched. This doesn't end when we reach the surface."

"So," said Densler, as he climbed up the ladder, "what is your backup plan anyways? You never told me."

"It's not a very good backup plan," said Patel. "Let's just wait until we see if that Humvee survived first."

Not a very good backup plan? thought Densler. *You mean compared to everything else that has gone on today? Peachy.*

Chapter 61

The Desert. 26 October 2009. 0946 Hours.

About three quarters of the way up the elevator shaft, the Jabberwocks stopped. Densler was on a landing when he looked down and noticed.

"Sarge," said Densler, "this looks promising. I think they're giving up."

Patel looked down at the Jabberwocks. Densler thought they looked even creepier just standing still. They were just above the next landing below them, silent and unmoving. Their green-lighted pinpoint eyes stared up at the men.

"Maybe," said Patel, "and maybe not. They haven't turned around and gone home yet, have they?"

"No," said Densler. "I guess not. Let's just get the hell out of here."

"Indeed," said Patel.

The two men again continued their ascent, Densler in the lead, Patel carrying the fuel. The Jabberwocks did not pursue. About five minutes later, they learned why.

THE DESERT

A sound echoed from deep below, reverberating against the earthen walls of the shaft. It sounded to Densler like a loud cough, but a little 'wet,' as if the person doing the coughing was dying of tuberculosis. Densler stopped.

"What the hell was that?" asked Densler.

"I don't know," said Patel. "It's nothing I've heard before. Now, get moving before I knock your ass off this ladder and out of my way."

The coughing sound happened again, this time joined by other, similar but fainter sounds.

Densler craned his neck down again and could see a slight commotion of illuminated green at the base of the shaft. "Now what?" asked Densler.

"Now I'm gonna put my boot in your ass if you don't move it, soldier!" shouted Patel.

The green figures at the bottom of the shaft began to appear larger and more distinct. Densler thought he could make out two separate entities, and they appeared to be moving upwards at a significant rate of speed.

"Oh, fuck!" said Densler. Then he began scrambling up the ladder.

"Dear God," said Patel, "let those be shades." He followed right behind Densler.

"They're not shades, Sarge," said Densler. "They have wings."

Chapter 62

The Desert. 26 October 2009. 1002 Hours.

As Densler approached the next landing, Patel shouted, "Stop at the landing and wait for me! We have to make a stand here!"

"Make a stand?" asked Densler. "With what? I forgot my holy water and Bible at home, Sarge!" He swung himself onto the next landing.

"If they aren't shades," said Patel, "then they can hurt us. If they can hurt us, then we can hurt them."

Patel climbed up onto the landing and removed the webgear and fuel canisters from his back. He pulled out the large hunting knife and crouched in an attack position. Densler followed suit and unsheathed his Ka-Bar.

The creatures rising through the elevator shaft were by now nearly upon them. They ascended slowly, yet with an almost beautiful fluidity. Although they did indeed have wings, they did not flap them in the manner of birds or bats, but rather appeared to be gliding upon an air current that did not exist within the confines of the elevator shaft.

Densler stepped back from the edge and crouched lower, holding his combat knife straight out in front of him. Patel was motionless, like a mountain lion poised to strike.

The first of the creatures passed the landing and glided to the wall to the left of Densler. It grabbed the wall with claws that jutted from the apex of the right wing where a bat's thumb would normally be located. However, unlike a bat, the wings appeared to have no fingers giving support, as the entire hand was external to the wing.

The majority of the creature was not visible to Densler at this time, as the left wing closed around the creature's body, shielding it from view. The wings were less like wings than pale, fleshy sheets hanging from the spindly arms. The creature hung there for a few moments, unmoving, while its sheet-like wings flapped in a nonexistent breeze.

Next, it tensed slightly and jumped from the wall to the landing, perching precariously on the metal railing. The creature spread its wings, uncovering a monstrous body even more hideous than the Jabberwocks. Its corpselike body was thin, the ribcage clearly defined under a nearly transparent layer of skin. The legs were short and crooked, as if deformed through some sort of physical infirmity. The feet looked vaguely human, yet they grasped the railing like a lower primate. The arms, from which draped the sheet-like wings, were long and frail, ending in short-fingered hands with long, scythe-like claws.

But the most gruesome aspect of the creature was its head. It hung low, in front of its ribs, on a two-foot long neck. Its head was little more than thin, clear skin clinging to the upper half of a human skull. There were no discernible teeth or a lower jaw. If the creature had eyes, then Densler could not see them. The eye sockets appeared merely empty holes. The head tracked from side to side gracefully.

Densler tried to back up, but found that he was already at the wall, the creature only three feet from him. Patel attacked the creature from Denler's right, swinging his knife in wide side-to-side motions. The blade connected with the creature's left wing, slicing through it as though it were paper.

The creature made the coughing sound they had heard earlier; only up close it was even viler. Flecks of black liquid sprayed from beneath the creature's skull-like head onto Densler's chest and legs.

Densler swung his Ka-Bar at the creature's head, and the blade bounced of the skull, knocking the head into the thing's right wing. Densler could see a rather large flap of pale skin hanging off of the head where he had slashed at it. The flap of skin floated up from the skull, defiantly resisting gravity in a fashion that was almost mesmerizing.

The fiend closed its wings around its body as if shielding itself from further blows. Patel struck downwards with his knife, sinking it deep into the creature's abdomen near its left shoulder. The monster spread its wings wide and tried to shove off from the railing, but Patel clung to the hunting knife's handle, still embedded to the hilt in its flesh.

The monster reached towards Patel with its left arm, spreading wide the curved blades of its claws. It ripped at Patel's right arm, and the sergeant let go of the knife. He dropped to the floor of the landing, clutching his wounded arm.

Chapter 63

The Desert. 26 October 2009. 1024 Hours.

Densler stepped forward to go to Patel and help him, but the second creature suddenly flew up over the railing and landed between the two men. It crouched and jumped at Densler, both of its vicious clawed hands splayed open towards him. Densler dropped backwards, attempting to flee the attack but accidentally falling through the opening where the ladder attached to the landing. His right leg and arm fell through the hole, but he caught himself with his left hand before dropping completely through.

The creature tripped over Densler's supine body and careened into the railing at the opposite end of the platform. It made a peculiar sound as it collapsed, like a bag of large sticks thrown to the ground. It made the horrid coughing sound, but this time it sounded almost plaintive, as if it was asking a question.

Densler pulled himself out of the hole and crouched, checking for any further attacks. The first creature was nowhere in sight, but the second one lay motionless at one corner of the landing. As he looked at it, it appeared to grow fainter, and within a few seconds, it disappeared like a dream image upon waking.

Patel stood up and cautiously peered over the side of the railing. He was still holding his injured right arm. It was hard to see clearly in the pale green mist, but Densler could tell that the sergeant was bleeding profusely from the wounds.

"Bad news," said Patel, quite calmly. "We're about to have more company."

Patel stepped back from the railing and went to the ladder. He started to try to climb the ladder with only one hand, but Densler could see that they were going to be much slowed down by the sergeant's injury. He frantically tried to think of a plan, something to slow down the attacks.

"Shit," said Patel, stepping back off the ladder. "You better go on ahead. I'll just slow you down."

"I have a better idea, Sarge," said Densler. "But I have a question for you? How far do you think we'd get on just one five-gallon can of gas?"

Chapter 64

The Desert. 26 October 2009. 1040 Hours.

Patel chuckled. "I see where you're going with that idea." He paused. "I guess we can try. It's not like we're even sure we'll be able to get any vehicle going, so I guess worrying about the gas is not exactly a number one priority. What's your plan?"

"We set one of the cans on the landing," said Densler. "Then when they get near the landing, I shoot it from above. The can explodes, hopefully killing them, but at least screwing up their vision."

"Well," said Patel, "I'd love to point out the flaws in your plan, but right now, we better get going. I guess I'll have to go first, since you are gonna have to shoot that rifle."

Patel moved up the ladder as fast as he could. Densler removed one of the cans from his web gear harness and set it on its side, so that it would present a larger target next to the ladder opening on the floor.

As Densler arranged his trap, he could see through the hole in the floor the *company* to which Patel had referred.

Apparently, the Jabberwocks had taken the opportunity of the flying creatures' attack to resume the chase and attempt to close the distance. He could see the horrible visage of the lead creature and its brightly glowing pinprick eyes. It approached from less than twenty feet.

If that fucker opens its mouth, thought Densler, *I'm a dead man.*

Densler scrambled up the ladder and climbed as fast as possible, catching up to Patel almost immediately. The sergeant had only progressed about thirty feet up the ladder.

"Hurry up, Sarge!" said Densler.

"I'm going as fast as I can," said Patel through gritted teeth.

Densler unslung his rifle from his shoulder and hooked his left arm around a ladder rung.

"Are you nuts?" asked Patel. "We're nowhere near far enough away for you to be firing that thing."

"They're almost here!" said Densler.

"Yeah," said Patel. "Almost. As in, not yet. You shoot now and you might not even singe them. Wait until they're around the platform."

"I'm nuts?" said Densler. "We let them get that close, and we can kiss our asses goodbye. What if one of them opens its mouth and makes that sound?"

"Just wait until they get around the platform," said Patel. "Trust me."

Patel and Densler slowly inched up the ladder. The wound on Patel's arm had stopped bleeding, but Densler could see that the sergeant was still in significant pain. A few times, Patel tried to use it, but had to stop, wincing and unable to flex his fingers.

THE DESERT

"How bad is your arm?" asked Densler.

"It's not good," said Patel. "I suppose that I should be thankful, though."

"Thankful?" said Densler. "Are you kidding?"

"Well," said Patel. "If that creature had been completely *here*, and by here I mean *in this world*, then it would have taken my arm clear off at the elbow. But since it's not *here*, it really fucked up my arm, but I think I'll recover."

"How so?" asked Densler, glad to have something to talk about.

"You see," said Patel, "since they aren't completely *here*, they can't interact materially the same way that you and I can. When it cut me, it slashed completely through my arm. However, since it wasn't altogether *here*, the slash was more like a dotted line than a complete one. It left large parts of my arm untouched as its claws passed through them."

"So how were we able to fight them off?" asked Densler.

"The one that I fought," said Patel, "I accidentally left my knife sticking out of it. I have a feeling that, since it stayed in the creature, that it caused enough damage to kill it. Did you see what happened to the second one?"

"Yeah," said Densler. "It tripped and fell, then disappeared."

"Exactly," said Patel. "When it tripped, it broke some of its bones. I heard them pop. When they receive any kind of significant damage, then their hold on this world is loosened. It didn't *die* because it fell and broke some bones, but it wasn't able to concentrate on staying material anymore. I liken it to treading water. It takes a great deal of energy to stay afloat, but once you get used to it, you can do it without devoting too much mental or physical attention to it. But if something happens to you, say you get a cramp or something...then you might drown or at least temporarily lose your rhythm."

"I hate to cut this short," said Densler, "but they're coming around the landing now. Brace yourself!"

"Get ready with the rifle!" said Patel, locking his good arm around a rung of the ladder.

Two of the Jabberwocks were now visible, each one on either side of the platform, climbing as fast as they could. One of them, the first one that had pursued them, began to open its malevolent jaws.

"Now, Densler!" said Patel. "Now!"

Chapter 65

The Desert. 26 October 2009. 1056 Hours.

Densler fired the assault rifle once. It created a loud popping sound in the cave, reverberating in the wide-open chasm. It produced enough of a muzzle flash to cause both men to momentarily lose their vision in the dark. However, it did not cause the fuel tank to explode.

"Dammit!" said Densler.

"Keep firing until you hit it!" said Patel.

Densler fired again, this time causing a tiny spark on the metal platform where the bullet struck. The Jabberwocks seemed confused by the light flashes and sound. They began to move outward from the platform.

"Hurry!" said Patel.

"I'm trying!"

Densler took a deep breath, and re-aimed at the fuel canister. He tried to remain calm and slowly squeezed on the trigger as he exhaled.

Although the resulting explosion was of a much smaller scale than would be expected in a Hollywood action film, it was significant enough to cause a great deal of havoc. There was a bright flash on the floor of the platform, and fiery diesel fuel blasted up and outwards.

Densler saw one of the Jabberwocks thrown from the wall during the explosion, then the bright flash temporarily blinded him. Before he could recover, there was a loud groaning sound, but it was not coming from a creature of any sort. It was a metallic groan issuing from the structure of ladders and platforms.

"Oh fuck!" said Patel.

"Hold on!" said Densler. "This is going to suck!"

There was a loud bang as the platform below them separated from the wall of the elevator shaft. The ladder that they were hanging on shifted and swung to the right slightly. More metallic groans echoed throughout the shaft, from both above and below.

"Move your ass, Sergeant!" said Densler.

Patel climbed as quickly as he could up the ladder towards the next landing. As they neared the landing, Densler could see that the ladder was beginning to separate from the platform. Patel swung onto the platform and rolled over to the side, ending up against the railing.

Densler reached through the opening of the platform and grabbed onto the metal grate floor. The ladder broke beneath him and twisted, now only clinging to the landing by one of its two supports. Densler pulled himself up onto the platform and laid flat on his back, panting and heaving due to the physical strain of the preceding events.

After pausing a few moments to catch his breath, Densler turned to look down the hole from which he had come. The ladder hung crookedly on its single support, and the platform below appeared to have fallen away, but the rest of the ladder system below them was still essentially intact.

THE DESERT

There was no sign of any of the creatures. Densler looked over at Patel and smiled.

"Don't," said Patel. "Not yet, anyway. We just bought a little time, that's all. It's not Miller time yet."

"Come on!" said Densler. "Did you see that shit? I blew the whole damned platform off the wall. Those jibber-jabber sacks of shit were blown back to Hell. Can't you just be optimistic for a moment?"

"I'd like to be," said Patel, "but the truth of the matter is this: number one, they don't need the ladders to get up here, since they walk up the side of the wall; number two, I'm pretty fucked up, and we're both tired as hell; and number three, you didn't kill any of the Jabberwocks."

"What do you mean I didn't kill them?" said Densler. "I saw one of them blown right off the side of the platform! The flying ones were easy enough to kill."

"I don't know anything about the flying ones," said Patel. "This is the first time I've ever seen those things. What I do know is that the Jabberwocks cannot be harmed like that. I don't know why. I told you before, we fired a rocket into one of them, and it didn't even seem to notice! You really think it gives a damn about a little bit of burning gasoline? We have to get moving."

Chapter 66

The Desert. 26 October 2009. 1127 Hours.

"Let me see your arm before we go," said Densler. "I have a first aid kit."

Densler removed the tiny kit from his web gear strap, which consisted of little more than a bit of bandage and a few pieces of gauze. Patel held his injured hand out towards him. The wound was very peculiar looking, and Densler hesitated a moment before wrapping it up in the bandages. Like Patel had said before, the wound was not a simple slash across his arm, but more like a jagged, dotted line. The creature had flashed between both worlds during the attack, and only when it was solid could it harm him. Densler wrapped the arm tightly, and tried not to think about the implications of fighting creatures that weren't completely *here*.

"Fucking crazy shit, huh?" said Patel. "I don't even want to think about what kinds of hellish infection I'm gonna get from fighting a...what's a good name for that piece of shit... uh, a *gargoyle*. Yeah, that's right, a gargoyle. I knew watching

THE DESERT

all those old monster movies would come in useful one day."

Patel was trying to lighten the mood, as soldiers often did in situations of extreme peril. But underneath the joking exterior, Densler recognized something that he had not as yet seen in the tough old sergeant: fear.

"How's that, Sarge?" asked Densler.

"It's actually a lot better," said Patel. "It still hurts like a son of a bitch, but I think I'll be able to use it a little bit to climb. That ought to speed us up somewhat, at least."

Patel started climbing up the ladder to the next platform, indeed slightly faster than before. Densler followed after, somewhat lighter now that only a single fuel canister weighed him down. The two men ascended in silence, and Densler was glad for it. The exertion was beginning to really take its toll on him. Densler concentrated on moving upward, promising himself that it was just a little further. He could hear Patel above him, grunting with the pain and effort of his ascent, and it echoed through the elevator shaft.

And then, there was another sound. Deep down in the green-tinged darkness below, a Jabberwock howled its horrible dual-toned sonic blast. It was far enough away that it did not affect Densler, apart from making his inner ear twinge slightly. A moment later, more Jabberwocks joined in, creating a cacophony of hideous aural assault.

Chapter 67

The Desert. 26 October 2009. 1146 Hours.

"Does that shit sound like it's getting louder to you, Densler?" asked Patel.

"Yeah, so?" said Densler.

"Look down," said Patel.

Densler looked down and saw that at the bottom of the shaft, as far down as he could see, the green mist had begun to glow brighter than he had yet seen it. It was still quite a ways down, and he could make out no detail, but it appeared to be roiling and churning, as if a small storm. In addition, to the turbulent movement, Densler noted with horror that it also appeared to be moving upwards.

No words were necessary. Both men climbed as quickly as possible towards the next platform.

After Patel swung onto the landing, he called out, "Ha-ha! This is the last platform! I can see the top of the ladder!"

"About fucking time!" said Densler.

Patel wasted no time in celebration and climbed the last section of ladder towards the surface. Densler swung

THE DESERT

onto the platform and beheld the same welcome sight, high up above, the end of the ladder-system.

Densler climbed so fast that he lost his footing and slipped, momentarily hanging by his hands only. He looked down to see where to place his feet and also saw that the storm of green mist was much closer now. It was about three platforms below them, and now that it was nearer, he could discern more clearly the nature of the storm. It was not the mist itself that whipped about in tempestuous violence. Rather, the *storm* was comprised of hundreds of ghostly apparitions, spinning about like a green hurricane.

Densler nearly flew up the ladder, spurred on by the frightening scene below and the ever-increasing decibels of the screaming cacophony. As Patel climbed over the edge of the elevator shaft, Densler noticed that the walls and ceiling of the shaft were now beginning to appear to move.

Densler saw with great horror that more phantasmal figures were materializing from the wall around him. Green-tinged hands slowly worked their way out of the earthen wall. Screaming faces pushed through the dirt, their fluid movements at once both surreal and terrifying. The hands reached for Densler's legs, but passed through them without effect.

Densler finally reached the top of the ladder and started to swing over onto the ground. A spectral hand reached out from the wall at the lip of the shaft and grabbed for Densler's foot. The hand passed partially through his foot, unable to take hold, but Densler also felt as if someone had punched his foot. It was just barely enough to knock him off balance. He slipped and landed on his chest, his upper half on solid ground and his waist and legs dangling over the abyss.

He reached for a handhold to pull himself forward and saw multiple hands reaching out from the dirt floor at him.

They did not have any significant force to hurt him, but they were interfering with his ability to grab onto anything or pull himself up.

Densler could see Patel running down the corridor, towards the doors leading into the locker room. He started to call out to him, but as he opened his mouth to yell, more spectral arms rose from the floor and pushed into his mouth, causing him to gag and cough.

Densler saw Patel reach the doors then turn around to see why Densler wasn't following. Patel turned and ran back to Densler, stepping high as if trying to keep away from the dreadful phantasms rising from the ground. Some of the arms had now been followed by heads and torsos as the figures climbed out from the dark earth.

Patel grabbed Densler's right arm and pulled him out with all of the force that he could muster. Densler got to his feet, and the two men ran for the doors. Around them, ghostly figures of the dead, of many ages, races, and centuries, freed themselves from the earth surrounding them.

Densler and Patel raced through the locker room and into the corridors leading out to the village. They could hear the storm approaching behind them, the screaming now at a level that threatened to deafen the two men. At last, they reached the ladder that led upwards to the shack. Patel bolted up the ladder, then waited to help pull Densler through. The two men raced out of the shack and into the bright daylight and menacing heat of the Iraqi desert. They didn't stop running until they were nearing the main entrance area of the village. Finally, Patel stopped running, and Densler stopped with him.

After waiting to catch his breath, Patel said, "Well, one mystery is solved."

"Huh?" asked Densler.

THE DESERT

"The Humvee," said Patel. "We know what happened to it now."

"What do you mean?" asked Densler. "We haven't gotten to where I parked it yet."

"No," said Patel, gesturing to some wreckage leaning up against one of the shacks. "But I'm guessing that over there is one of its tires. Time to shoot for Plan B."

PART SIX

The Long March

Chapter 68

The Desert. 26 October 2009. 1213 Hours.

Densler sat down on the hood of the wrecked Humvee, which due to the fact that the vehicle no longer had any wheels, was much lower to the ground than normal. He ran his hands through his short, blonde hair and wiped his brow.

"So, Sarge," said Densler, "You said something about a Plan B?"

Patel pulled an empty 55-gallon drum over and sat down upon it. He placed his wounded hand in his lap, and took a deep breath.

"When we first arrived here," said Patel, "there was this truck that we found here being used as a gate, blocking the entrance. When our vehicles were damaged during the first night, I sent two men, Henson and Taylor, out into the desert with a radio to try and get out of the range of what we thought was jamming and radio for help."

"Okay," said Densler.

THE DESERT

"Well," said Patel. "Obviously, they didn't make it. But somewhere out there, the truck ran out of gas, and they died of starvation."

"How do you know the...demons...didn't get them?" asked Densler. "How do you know they didn't destroy the truck?"

"I don't," said Patel. "Not for certain, anyways. But what I do know is that neither Henson's nor Taylor's body was used by the demons."

"How would you know that?" asked Densler.

"I've accounted for the bodies of every single other one of my platoon, save Henson, Taylor, and Forbes. And since you told me where you found Forbes, I now believe that there is a chance that Henson and Taylor died without the intervention of the demons.

"I think the bastards don't like to go too far out into the desert at night. In fact, I've been thinking about it and I'll bet that the vast openness of the desert reminds them too much of the solid earth that they are trying to break free from. Besides, the Jabberwocks move so slowly that it would take them more than a single night to find them, and they are probably not too keen on being stuck, blinded by the sun out in the middle of the desert."

"Even if you're right," said Densler, "how can you be sure that the truck will still run after sitting out there for six years?"

"Hey," said Patel, with a little grin, "I didn't say it was a *good* plan. It's just all we have left. Besides, that truck was a workhorse. It started up pretty easily before, and who knows how long it had been sitting out here before we came upon it. I mean, look at this piece of shit village. It was just as deserted six years ago. It doesn't appear that anyone has been here in a lot longer than just six years."

"So we're just going to wander around in the desert, looking for a truck that could be, well...anywhere?"

"We have some pretty good ideas, actually," said Patel. "For example, we know you and Henderson didn't see it coming in, right?"

Densler nodded assent.

"Okay," said Patel. "We also know in what direction they left in, since I was the one who sent them away. We also know they didn't end up behind the village because it's as flat as a pancake back there for miles and miles. We'd see a glint off of something metal if they were out there somewhere. Given the amount of gas they had, and all of the facts that we do know, I'd estimate they are..." Patel pointed to a ridge in the distance. "I'd say somewhere right of that ridge to about where the land rises up and makes a high point before the road. You wouldn't be able to see that area from the road."

"That area encompasses quite a lot of acreage, Sarge."

"You got a better idea?" asked Patel.

Densler was silent.

"Didn't think so," said Patel. "We're gonna need to pack every bit of food and water we can carry. We're also gonna need the tool kit from the Humvee, and any oil, transmission fluid, or anything else like that, that you can scrounge up. Time's a wasting. We only have seven hours until dusk."

Chapter 69

The Desert. 26 October 2009. 1346 Hours.

An hour later, Densler had laid out a significant cache of supplies for the trek. He knew that there was too much for them to carry, especially with Patel injured, but he was not thrilled with the idea of having to leave any of it, especially the food and water, behind.

A rhythmic squeaking sound in the distance caused Densler to become alarmed. He turned around to see Patel coming around a corner with a wheelbarrow. It was crafted from old trey wood, and the wheel itself appeared to have been beaten out of iron by a blacksmith.

"Jesus, Sarge," said Densler. "If that ain't the crappiest wheelbarrow I ever did see."

Patel smiled and said, "It's not pretty, but it will do what we need it to do."

"Good thing, too," said Densler, "'cause I hate to leave any of this lovely smorgasbord of Army food behind."

Patel examined the supplies. He picked up an MRE and read off the contents.

"Spaghetti and meat sauce!" said Patel. "You are high speed, my friend. It's the only MRE I can stomach. Wait a second, you have like ten MREs here...and they're all spaghetti?"

"Yeah, Sarge," said Densler, "It's not so much because of the spaghetti that I stashed them in my Hummer. It's more because of the M&Ms inside each one. You always know, if it's a spaghetti MRE, you're getting M&Ms."

"Okay," said Patel, holding up a red, white & blue candy bar. "Now would you mind telling me what the fuck is a *Hooahh Bar*?"

"They're good for you, Sarge," said Densler. "Hooahh?"

"Let's just get all this shit in the wheelbarrow so we can get underway."

Fifteen minutes later, the wheelbarrow was packed with MREs, containers of water, the five-gallon fuel can, tools from the Humvee and other vehicles, a hand-cranked air pump, and bottles of motor oil, transmission fluid, and WD-40. Densler tentatively lifted the handles and moved it forward, listening to the creaking of the boards with suspicion.

"Well, Sarge," said Densler. "I guess we're about as ready as we'll ever be. I don't really trust this wheelbarrow though. I hope it lasts."

"It better," said Patel, "'cause I don't have a Plan C."

Chapter 70

The Desert. 26 October 2009. 1946 Hours.

By dusk, they were about halfway to the ridge. The region featured a significant amount of high and low areas that obscured much of the surrounding territory, making it very hard to search from the ground.

"Look at the bright side, Sarge," said Densler. "At least it won't be so hot for much longer."

"I like that you're an optimist, Densler," said Patel. "I never would have kept sane all these years if I hadn't been one myself. In fact, I was thinking about your theory about the afterlife, and I think in some ways it all boils down to optimism and pessimism."

"How so?" asked Densler.

"A pessimist has already decided that the existence of an afterlife is impossible. They've resigned themselves to the idea that when they die, all is lost. Poof. They cease to be, as if they never were."

"But all religious or spiritual people are optimists, especially agnostics. Unless you have experienced something truly supernatural."

"Like us?" interjected Densler.

"Yes," said Patel. "Like us. Unless you've seen some proof that there is something beyond death, then of course you are just basing that belief on faith. And what is faith if not optimism?"

"I see what you mean, Sergeant," said Densler.

"You know what, Densler?" asked Patel. "It's about time to stop that shit. Technically, I'm not even in the Army anymore. We've been through enough to call each other by our given names. You can call me Mahabala."

"And you can call me Specialist Densler," said Densler.

"Oh come on, son," said Patel. "You can't like the Army that much. I mean, look at you. You're what? Thirty years old? And still an E-4?"

"Actually," said Densler, "I'm twenty-nine. Besides, I don't want to be in charge of anyone. I'm not going to take the promotion board until they force me to do it. But I'm just happy to leave my name as it is, thank you."

"Seriously, Densler," said Patel. "I had no idea you were this uptight."

"It's not that, Sarge. It's just.... Aw, hell. My name's Hasil."

"Hasil?" asked Patel.

"It's a Southern name," said Densler. "You don't see it much on people that wear shoes."

"Oh don't be that way," said Patel. "Do I look like a guy that gives a damn about stereotypes? If I did, I guess I would have listened to my dad and became Mahabala Patel, M.D.

THE DESERT

or opened a convenience store. Besides, I like the name Hasil Densler. It makes you sound like an outlaw."

"Off the subject," said Densler, "I was kind of hoping we'd make it to the ridge, since that would probably be a good place to camp for the night."

"I agree," said Patel. "But we're not gonna make it there before nightfall. It's not gonna be easy dragging that wheelbarrow uphill either."

"I guess we better hurry then," said Densler.

Chapter 71

The Desert. 26 October 2009. 2016 Hours.

The sun set very differently in the desert on October 26, 2009. As the yellow orb of the sun dipped toward the horizon, it appeared to become less distinct and more blurred to the two men trudging across the desert. Had they been ordinary travelers on an ordinary excursion, this minor detail would have been of little consequence, and they would most likely have dismissed it as a meteorological irregularity of no great significance.

But since the two men were not ordinary travelers, they did notice the strange solar peculiarity. They observed the descending sun with alarm for more than one reason, as it also heralded the approach of the fiends who pursued them.

Spurned on by the onset of night, the two men traveled faster across the barren sand and rock, determined to put as much distance as possible between themselves and their gruesome adversaries.

THE DESERT

But the sun was neither an ally nor an enemy and did not take pity on the two men hurrying towards the ridge. It disappeared beyond the horizon in a fashion that appeared most bewildering to the men. As it lowered beyond the curvature of the Earth, it appeared distorted by a haze of green. The haze rippled like the illusions created by extreme heat. And most disconcerting of all, as soon as the sun disappeared, so did nearly all of the light.

The sky was almost instantly dark, as if unseen clouds rushed to blot out any remaining trace of sunlight. There were no stars visible, and within only fifteen minutes after sunset, the world had become almost entirely pitch black for Specialist Densler and Sergeant Patel.

Behind them, sounds already began to echo from the village. The hateful screams of the dead mingled with the horrible howls and coughs of the other creatures they had thus far encountered.

On previous nights, the green mist had slowly seeped into the village. But tonight, there was an eruption issuing forth from the center of the settlement. It curled upwards, moving more like a liquid than a gas before dispersing and settling to the ground below. It pressed towards the two fleeing men as though it were the leading edge of a luminous green avalanche.

It had taken Densler and Patel three hours to travel a little more than halfway to the safety of the ridge. The green mist had covered the same distance in thirty seconds. They were out of time.

Chapter 72

The Desert. 26 October 2009. 2034 Hours.

Densler broke into a jog, still pushing the wheelbarrow. The equipment inside rattled, and the wood planks holding the contraption together creaked and groaned.

"Don't jog unless you're sure you can keep that pace up, Densler!" shouted Patel, jogging alongside him. "We have miles to go yet, and I can't push that thing if you crap out on me."

"Sarge!" said Densler. "We don't have a choice! They'll be on us any second now! Look how fast that fucking mist got to us!"

"Calm down," said Patel. "We're so far ahead right now that it will take them quite awhile to get out here. The Jabberwocks move so slowly, I wouldn't even worry about them. Besides, like I said before, I don't think they're gonna want to come out too much farther. They'll just get lost out here, blind in the sunlight."

Densler slowed back down to a fast walk. He panted heavily.

THE DESERT

"See what I mean?" said Patel. "If you'd have kept jogging like that, pushing all that crap around, you wouldn't have lasted another half hour, much less the probable three to four hours we have left on this little sojourn. When you let fear overtake you, and panic governs your actions, you are no longer an effective soldier. You become little more than a militiaman with a hunting rifle. Order and discipline are what makes a soldier effective, not brute strength or fear. It's how a little city full of short Italian guys nearly conquered the whole world. Discipline."

"Right," said Densler. "But how is that going to help us get to that ridge?"

"Think about it, Densler," said Patel. "The majority of those spooks back there are either completely harmless shades or they can only slightly affect you, like the ones we encountered on our way out. Either way, discipline wins the day. We ignore the shades and we keep walking when the other ones push or pull us. It may sound simple, but as long as we keep our forward momentum, I think we can make it to the ridge before midnight. And if the hypothesis holds, and the mist can't follow us up there...well, let's just say that I'm kind of looking forward to a few hours of sleep tonight."

Chapter 73

The Desert. 26 October 2009. 2140 Hours.

The first hour following sunset was fairly uneventful. The screams and howls continued to sound in the distance, but every time Densler looked back towards the village, he saw no signs of pursuit. He began to become cautiously optimistic about the chances that they would make it to the ridge unmolested. However, at around 2145 hours, Densler looked back towards the village and saw something he most assuredly did not want to see.

"Sarge," said Densler, "we're about to have some company!"

Patel followed Densler's prompt. Densler set down the wheelbarrow and stood next to him.

"What are they?" asked Densler.

"Gargoyles," replied Patel. "Those flying things we fought in the elevator shaft. They're keeping low to stay inside of the fog, but that's definitely what they are."

"Fuck," said Densler.

THE DESERT

"Indeed," said Patel. "But we do know one thing about them. They're fragile and easy to hurt. Hand me your rifle."

"Are you sure you can shoot?" asked Densler.

"I can shoot better than I can push that wheelbarrow, which is what I need you to do right now. Besides, all my right hand needs to do is pull this trigger. I can manage that much."

Densler took the rifle off of his back and handed it to Patel. He also took the remaining six thirty-round magazines and placed them out on top of some supplies in the wheelbarrow so that Patel could reach them more easily. Then he began pushing the wheelbarrow again towards the ridge, though not feeling particularly happy about not being able to see what was going on behind him. Patel walked backwards behind Densler, holding the rifle and preparing for battle.

"How many would you estimate there are, Sarge?" asked Densler.

"Do you really want to know?" asked Patel.

"Yeah," said Densler.

"Let's put it this way," said Patel, "I might have enough ammo to take them out. Might."

That doesn't sound encouraging, thought Densler.

Chapter 74

The Desert. 26 October 2009. 2202 Hours.

It took the creatures almost a half-hour to catch up to the two men. They floated slowly upon the air, their flight more akin to that of a manta ray cutting through the ocean. They did not flap their wings, as a bird or bat might, nor did they appear to be affected by the wind, or in this case, the lack of it. The first of the creatures came to within thirty feet of the men, and Patel fired.

"Fuck!" said Patel.

"What is it, Sarge?" asked Densler, craning his neck around to see what was going on.

"Goddamned muzzle flash!" said Patel. "When I fire at the things, I can't tell if I hit it, because the muzzle flash kills my night vision."

"Then just keep firing!" said Densler. "Maybe it messes with them, too!"

Densler pushed the wheelbarrow as fast as he could without jogging or running. He could hear the sounds of Patel shooting the AR-15 and see the light caused by the

THE DESERT

muzzle flash, but he could not tell how good or bad a job Patel was doing back there.

The inability to monitor his situation was infuriating, but there was little he could do to rectify the situation. Whenever he craned his neck around to see what was going on, he ran the risk of losing control of the wheelbarrow, which was hard enough to steer at present.

Suddenly, one of the creatures landed on the front of the wheelbarrow, causing it to tip forward and capsize, dumping the contents onto the desert floor. Densler, urged forward by momentum, fell into the pile of equipment.

The creature lay on its back, with the fuel can on top of it. It reached out with its right arm/wing and slashed at Densler. Densler pushed back, narrowly avoiding being disemboweled by the bladed claws. He bumped into Patel, nearly knocking him down.

"Shoot that thing!" said Densler.

"No way!" said Patel. "I might hit the fuel."

Patel walked around the creature, giving it a wide berth. He stopped a few feet away from its head, and holding his rifle backwards like a club, proceeded to bash the gargoyle's skull with it. After three hits, the creature coughed and was silent.

Densler stood and looked around him. Gargoyles circled around them at a safe distance of about forty feet. The bodies of a few of the creatures were strewn out behind him, coughing their horrible, sickly, retching sounds.

"Help me get this stuff back in the wheelbarrow!" said Patel.

"Why are they staying so far away?" asked Densler.

"I think the muzzle flashes are confusing them," said Patel. "As long as I pop one of them every so often, they seem to stay out at a distance like that. This kamikaze son of a bitch was the exception." Patel gestured at the creature whose head he had just caved in. It was slowly disappearing into the desert sand. "Let's get going before they get any better ideas."

Chapter 75

The Desert. 26 October 2009. 2358 Hours.

They reached the base of the ridge just before midnight. Densler had to struggle hard to get the wheelbarrow up the first part of the formation. Up close, it appeared that what they had assumed was a mountainous ridge, was little more than a ridge-shaped hill. This was a fortuitous occurrence, however, as an actual ridge would have been more difficult to ascend.

After rising fairly steeply for about twenty feet, the ridge climbed at a low acute angle towards an apex about a half-mile away. Densler was intensely grateful for this, as it made the wheelbarrow much easier to push than at the beginning of the ridge. About halfway towards the apex, Patel stopped.

"Densler," said Patel. "It looks to me like we're safe for the moment."

Densler looked back down the ridge. The ceiling of the green mist was plainly visible below them. Off in the distance, he could see the village, still glowing brighter than anything else in the desert. About a third of the way from the village to the ridge, something approached which alarmed him.

"Sarge," said Densler. "Do you see them there?"

"Yeah," said Patel. "Don't worry about those Jabberwocks. Even if they walk all night, they won't make it to the ridge before the sun comes up. Even if they did, they'd be totally blind up here. I guess it just shows that they really aren't that smart."

"Okay," said Densler. "I guess you're right."

"Don't worry about them," said Patel. "Get some sleep. I have first watch. I'll be waking your ass up in three hours, so make sure you make them count!"

Densler laid himself out on the dusty incline and tried to get comfortable. He felt so wired and tense that he contemplated asking Patel to switch with him so he could take first watch.

I'll never fall asleep with those things out there slowly plodding their hideous looking bodies towards me, thought Densler. *What the hell are you thinking? I might as well try to find something useful to do with my time other than sleep.*

And then, against his better judgment, and in spite of the stress and adrenalin coursing through his veins, Specialist Densler succumbed to sleep.

Chapter 76

The Desert. 27 October 2009. 0300 Hours.

True to his word, Patel woke Densler almost exactly three hours later. At first, Densler thought he hadn't slept at all, until Patel spoke to him.

"Okay, son," said Patel. "Your turn for watch. The sun should rise around 0600, but if that green shit disappears before then, get me up. We're gonna need every spare minute tomorrow."

Densler looked at his watch and discovered he had indeed slept for three hours, which more than surprised him. He stood up and stretched, then paced around for a few moments, making sure he was awake enough to be alert.

He looked off in the distance at the slow approach of the Jabberwocks. He wished he could get a better look at them so that he could understand a little more about what exactly they were. Suddenly, he remembered that Patel had put a pair of binoculars into the wheelbarrow to help them search for the truck.

Densler rummaged through the supplies until he found them. Then he found a rather large boulder and sat down upon it, so that he could watch the approach of the horrid creatures.

Once he had adjusted the binoculars and sighted on the creatures, he was almost sorry that he had. Although the optics weren't strong enough to make out significant details on the demonic monsters, they were still the most horrible things that he had ever seen.

There were ten of them, walking in a ragged horizontal line. Their one-foot-at-a-time, plodding walk reminded him of something, but he couldn't quite remember what it was. Then it hit him and he chuckled.

This is like that scene in The Empire Strikes Back, he thought. *They move just like the Imperial walkers. God, I must be an idiot to be chuckling about this right now.*

Then something happened that chilled him to the bones. The lead creature, the chattering, shivering one that he had seen before, stopped. Then all of the other creatures followed suit.

The chattering Jabberwock turned its massive head and looked straight at him. Its tiny, glowing eyes appeared to fix on him from an enormous distance away. It opened its lurid mouth, exposing its macabre assortment of nearly transparent teeth.

Even at this extreme distance, the sound of its howl was so repellent that Densler nearly dropped the binoculars. He set them down and decided against any further observation of the creatures.

Chapter 77

The Desert. 27 October 2009. 0524 Hours.

As Densler approached Patel to wake him, the sergeant opened his eyes.

"Oh," said Densler. "You're awake."

"I heard you coming," said Patel. He sat up. "Anything interesting occur during the night?"

"I, uh, watched the Jabberwocks a little bit," said Densler. "There were ten of them, and they knew that I was watching them."

"I figured as much when I heard that howling crap last night," said Patel. "They never cease to amaze. Did they ever turn back?"

"No," said Densler. "They were about halfway here when the green fog finally dissipated too much to see them."

"Plucky bastards they are," said Patel. "They don't give up easily, do they?"

"So," said Densler, "do you have any idea which way we should look for the truck?"

"Oh indeed I do," said Patel, grinning. "I'm looking right at it."

Densler turned around and down below them in the distance he could see the approaching sunlight glinting off of something metal.

"Hot damn," said Densler.

"Hot damn indeed," said Patel. "We need to get moving though, cause we're only gonna have one day to get this right. We can't push that truck up this hill if we can't get it fixed. When we get to the truck, we'll take turns having a quick breakfast, while the other works on the truck. Sound like a plan to you?"

"Sounds truly peachy, Sarge."

Chapter 78

The Desert. 27 October 2009. 0738 Hours.

As Densler and Patel approached the truck, their hearts sank. All four tires were flat, and the vehicle was not in very good condition. The truck looked to Densler like its best years had occurred about forty years ago.

"A UNIMOG?" asked Densler.

"Dependable vehicles, aren't they?" said Patel.

Densler was hardly an expert, but the truck looked like a mid-sixties Mercedes-Benz UNIMOG (UNIversal-MOtor-Gerät) military truck, a multi purpose truck with a distinctive van-like front hood. It was painted beige, like pretty much every military vehicle in the Middle East. It didn't have a closed cabin, just a windshield. The left side of the truck looked pretty beat up, with much of its exterior ripped apart.

"We did the damage to it on the left side," said Patel. "It had that silly metal wall attached to it there, and I didn't want my guys lugging an extra couple hundred pounds of steel around the desert. Damn things only get about ten miles per gallon on a good day as it is."

As they reached the truck, Patel jogged ahead and checked inside and under the vehicle.

"Looks like Henson and Taylor didn't stick with the truck," said Patel. "Who knows where they ended up out here. At least they didn't end up as ghouls. You know anything about diesel engines?"

"Only that they're pretty dependable," said Densler. "I had a friend who drove one of those old Mercedes 300Ds around, and he used to brag that he was closing in on five hundred thousand miles and hadn't spent a dime on mechanics in two years."

"Well," said Patel. "I guess I'm gonna be pulling mechanic duty today. I've worked on Humvees before. This can't be too dissimilar."

Densler parked the wheelbarrow near the front of the vehicle. He walked around it and looked it over.

"You know, Sarge," said Densler. "I think you overlooked something. There's no way this puppy's battery is gonna still be charged."

"Oh I know," said Patel. "That's why they come with these handy gadgets." The sergeant held up a hand crank that he had just pulled out from under the front seat. "Since my arm's fucked, it looks like *you're* the battery."

THE DESERT

Chapter 79

The Desert. 27 October 2009. 1244 Hours.

"Densler," said Patel. "I think I'm gonna have to work on this engine a lot more than I thought."

"You think?" asked Densler.

"Funny guy," said Patel. "That's why you're gonna start working on the wheels."

"Shouldn't we wait until later? So the air stays in them long enough for us to get out of here?"

"Son," said Patel. "How long do you think it's gonna take you to pump those massive tires up by hand? Trust me, you better get started if you want to be done before nightfall."

Densler retrieved the hand pump from the wheelbarrow and got to work. Needless to say, hand-pumping air into truck tires in the middle of a desert around noon was not exactly a fun or relaxing situation. But Densler worked himself into a rhythm, switching hands when they became fatigued and even trying not to slow down when he drank water.

Back before he joined the Army, Densler used to like monotonous jobs like this. He remembered with fondness his first real job, running the broiler at Burger King.

The BK broiler is about the most mind-numbingly simple job in all of fast food. Basically, you just stand at the rear of it and feed in cold hamburger patties. Seconds later, they come out, fully cooked, on the other side where you then place them between hamburger buns.

Densler loved that job. He didn't have to devote so much as a single brain cell to the operation of that broiler. He could be thinking about anything: a favorite song; a book he was reading; or even a movie he'd love to see made. About the only thing he refused to let his mind drift towards was sex. He absolutely did not want to be seen standing at the broiler in a state of sexual turgidity. Imagine the rumors that such a thing could have encouraged.

So it was no surprise to Densler that he was much happier pumping up the tires than working on the engine, which would have required significantly more mental consciousness. After a while, he started singing Army cadences in his head.

"Hey Sarge," said Densler. "Mind if I sing some cadences?"

"Go ahead," said Patel. "As long as the word *dothead* doesn't pop up in any of them."

However, the kinds of cadences that Densler preferred were far more of the *black comedy* variety, particularly those which dealt with maniacal killing and ridiculous sexual exploits. He opened with the most infamous of Vietnam-era cadences:

We shoot the sick, the young, the lame,
We do our best to maim,
Because the kills all count the same,
Napalm sticks to kids.

THE DESERT

Patel dropped his wrench into the engine and banged his head on the open hood of the truck. He looked around the vehicle at Densler, laughing hysterically, tears streaming from his eyes.

"Holy shit, son," he said. "I haven't laughed so hard in six years!"

"Oh don't worry, Sarge," said Densler. "I'm a regular collector of sicko cadences. After I get done with this one I'll do *Strafe the Town and Kill the People* for you. And when I run out of cadences, I'll start on sea shanties. I know thirty verses of the *Good Ship Venus!*"

For once, the desert echoed with the sound of laughter rather than the screams of the hateful dead and the howls of grim Jabberwocks.

Chapter 80

The Desert, 27 October 2009, 1920 Hours.

As the sun lowered towards the horizon and darkness approached, the jovial atmosphere of the afternoon disappeared and was replaced with an ominous foreboding. Although Densler had completed pumping up the tires an hour ago, he now had to refill each tire constantly as air leaked out. But even more importantly, Patel had yet to get the engine to crank.

"Damn this German piece of shit!" said Patel. "I just don't get what its problem is."

"Well, just put a lot of WD-40 on everything and let's try to crank it again."

Ten minutes later, Patel came back from the front of the vehicle. "I'm gonna try it again," he said. "Load up our equipment before I do, because I think I might have to keep it revved up if it starts. I'd rather be moving forward than wasting gas in one place."

THE DESERT

Densler loaded the supplies into the cab of the truck and threw the now empty fuel can into its rear cargo bed. Patel sat down in the driver's seat, and Densler got in front with the hand crank.

"Hold on to your ass," said Densler. "Here goes."

Densler cranked the handle as fast as he could. The engine coughed a little, then stopped.

"Well," said Densler. "That's the best we've gotten so far."

"Yeah," said Patel. "But it ain't good enough. Let's try it a couple more times though. I think the fuel must be at least getting to the engine now."

On the second try, the engine coughed harder. Thick smoke poured out of the tailpipe.

"Keep cranking!" said Patel, furiously pumping the gas pedal.

Finally, the engine puttered into life. It sounded horrible, like a Panzer tank on its last legs, but to Patel and Densler, the rattling old engine meant that there was a glimmer of hope.

"Get in!" yelled Patel, revving the engine up to keep it from stalling.

Densler grabbed the crank from the front of the engine and jumped up into the passenger seat. As he slammed the door, Patel shifted into first gear and started the old truck forward. He turned right so that the village was directly behind them.

"I'm gonna drive slow," said Patel. "With only five gallons of fuel and this thing's shitty miles-per-gallon, we're gonna need to conserve as much as possible. Get the rope ready so we can tie the steering wheel off."

"You're still convinced we need to do that?" asked Densler.

"This whole thing will be for nothing if we just drive around in circles," said Patel. "We only have about five hours of driving left on this thing as is. Let's make sure they count."

"And what if we run into anything out here?" asked Densler.

"We won't," said Patel. "Remember how long it took last night for the Jabberwocks to make it anywhere near us? We might have to shoot some of those flying shitheads, so be ready. But that's all I'm worried about. Hand me that jarhead knife of yours. That's all the protection I need."

As Densler tied the rope around the steering wheel, locking it in position, the sun disappeared on the far horizon ahead of them.

Chapter 81

The Desert. 27 October 2009. 2005 Hours.

Patel flipped the switch for the headlights. The right headlight did not come on at all. The left one flickered, and then stayed off.

"Great," said Patel. "And I'll bet its gonna get real dark again tonight. Let's just hope we get away from this accursed area before that fog crap rolls in."

"Sarge," said Densler. "I wouldn't waste too much time hoping for that." He was turned around in the seat, holding the AR-15. "It looks like that green shit is rolling toward us as fast as it did last night. It's looks like a radioactive dust storm. Jesus."

The green fog flew towards them, creeping over the desert sand with speed and efficiency. In only a few moments, it was already catching up to the truck.

"But still," said Patel, "the demons will just be leaving the village now. We ought to have plenty of time before..."

"Fucking Christ!" yelled Densler. "Jabberwock! Fifteen feet behind us!"

As the green fog reached the UNIMOG, it illuminated the demon, walking perpendicular to their progress. It was the closest that Densler had come to one of the creatures. The way it moved was almost graceful, its long waxen limbs slowly propelling the hideous creature forward. The thin, gauzelike trails of sallow flesh trailing from its body defied gravity. It stopped and swung its enormous ghastly head towards the truck.

"How in the hell?" yelled Patel, stepping on the gas.

"They must have wandered around last night!" said Densler. "They didn't go back to the village. They're already here!"

THE DESERT

Chapter 82

The Desert. 27 October 2009. 2012 Hours.

As the fog rolled out beyond them, towards the darkened horizon, their situation appeared even more dire. The Jabberwock was not alone, as it appeared that all ten of them had wandered around the area, silently awaiting nightfall. Directly ahead of them, the chattering one waited.

It crouched low, like a tiger preparing to pounce. It opened its mouth wide, its jaws shivering.

"Turn!" said Densler. "Get us out of here!" He reached over and grabbed the steering wheel, but the rope was tied too tightly. It would not budge. Patel shifted into second gear and stepped on the gas, bringing the lumbering vehicle up to about twenty-five miles per hour.

"I can't!" said Patel. "Brace yourself!"

At a distance of approximately ten feet from the creature, it unleashed its terrible roar upon them. All thoughts of trying to turn the vehicle were brushed aside. The only thing that Densler was conscious of was the sound. The horrible sound blotted out all of his thoughts. His head exploded with pain, and his body shook as if experiencing a seizure.

Densler put his hands to the sides of his head and felt warm blood oozing between his fingers. He ducked down and waited for the pain to pass, and then vomited into the floorboards of the cab.

Although the pain seemed to last forever, the sound suddenly ceased after only a few seconds. Densler looked up at Patel and saw blood running from his ears. Densler finally noticed that they didn't appear to have hit anything, as he had felt no impact.

"What happened?" yelled Densler.

"I can't hear you!" replied Patel.

Densler sat back up in his seat and looked ahead. The Jabberwock was no longer in front of them, but others were attempting to pursue them from the sides.

"We drove through the fucker!" yelled Patel. "It was like driving through smoke! It just dissipated as we hit it!"

Densler turned around in the seat and saw that the chattering Jabberwock was behind them now, as if it had become whole again. It was marching as fast as it could behind them, but at such a slow pace it would never catch up to the truck.

But as Densler kept his eyes on the beast, something changed. It started to become brighter and it began to have less trouble walking. It started to look more solid than before, its pale skin becoming gradually more real and less spectral. All of a sudden, the shreds of skin that had hung suspended in the air now submitted to gravity and fell. The creature then began to gallop forward, almost like a horse, at a much higher speed than any of the Jabberwocks had previously been able to muster. It chattered its gruesome jaws together, and for the first time, this appeared to Densler to be the way the creature laughed.

THE DESERT

Somehow, the creature had become solid, totally on this side of the two worlds, and because of this, it was able to move faster. It was closing on them.

Chapter 83

The Desert. 27 October 2009. 2013 Hours.

"Oh fuck!" said Densler. He scrambled to aim the rifle out the back of the cab.

"What are you shooting at?" yelled Patel.

"It's running at us!" shouted Densler.

"What?" asked Patel.

Densler pointed behind them. Patel twisted around to see what Densler was pointing at, momentarily letting some pressure off of the gas pedal. The vehicle slowed down to about twenty miles per hour. Patel looked behind the truck, then twisted back around and floored the pedal.

The Jabberwock was now steadily overtaking them, only five feet behind the rear cargo bed of the truck. Densler fired at it, wildly shooting from the hip. Most of the shots missed the creature, but a few hit it, going through the creature and leaving little damage. It did not bleed, nor did it seem to experience any pain as a result of the gunshot wounds. It just continued to gain on them with horrific ferocity.

Click!

THE DESERT

Densler's rifle was now empty. He turned back around in his seat to find the next magazine, but all of their equipment, including the ammo, was now rolling around on the floorboard of the truck's cab.

He grabbed the first magazine he could find, barely noticing that it was covered in his own puke, and rammed it into the AR-15. He cocked the rifle and turned back around to face the monster.

As he turned around, the rear of the truck lurched, and Densler felt an uneasy sense of foreboding. His worst fears were realized as he now saw that the Jabberwock had reached the vehicle and jumped onto the rear cargo bed. Its huge head reached forward on its slender neck, now only a couple feet away from Densler.

Densler leaned over to Patel and screamed as loud as he had ever screamed into the man's damaged ears, "Brakes!"

Chapter 84

The Desert. 27 October 2009. 2014 Hours.

Patel looked at him, still unable to understand what he was saying.

Densler screamed again, "Hit the fucking brakes!"

Apparently, Patel finally understood what was being asked of him and he removed his foot from the accelerator and slammed down upon the brakes. The vehicle's wheels locked, and the UNIMOG fishtailed slightly to the right as it came to a stop. The Jabberwock flew over the cab, landing in a heap fifteen feet in front of the truck. The truck stalled and shut off.

"Is it dead?" asked Patel.

The creature did not move. It lay on its side, its limbs splayed out. The creature's head was not visible from this position.

Patel tried to start the truck, but the motor did not make a sound. He slammed his fist into the steering wheel.

"Fucking starter motor must be disconnected or something!" said Patel. "I didn't even worry about it because

THE DESERT

I didn't think we'd need it. You're gonna have to go out there and crank it."

"Fuck," said Densler.

He searched around the floor for the hand crank and finally found it. He then handed the rifle to Patel.

"Cover me," said Densler. "If that thing so much as moves, empty the magazine!"

Patel nodded, though Densler wondered if he had heard a single word. Densler slowly got out of the truck, looking around for signs of the other Jabberwocks. He could see some of them back the way they had come, but they were still pretty far away.

As long as they don't get any ideas about doing the same thing as this one, thought Densler, *we might have a chance of getting away from here.*

He walked over to the front of the vehicle and crouched, placing the hand crank back into the front of the engine. He turned so that he could see the Jabberwock while he worked, then began to furiously crank the engine.

The engine sputtered and started, then as Patel put the rifle down between the seats, it coughed and stalled again. Densler started to crank the engine again, as fast as he possibly could, and the engine finally started again. This time, it stayed running. Densler jogged back around to the passenger door and climbed in.

As Densler pulled himself into the vehicle, Patel watched him to see when he could put the UNIMOG in gear. Both men turned forward and looked ahead as Patel shifted into first.

In the few seconds that they had taken their eyes away from the Jabberwock, it had silently risen to its feet, and now it stood in front of the truck, chattering its ghastly laugh.

Patel slammed down the gas pedal, but the old diesel engine was painfully slow to accelerate. The creature crept to the driver's left, out of the way of the vehicle, and crouched, preparing to attack.

Patel leaned over toward the passenger's side, anticipating the attack, and Densler scrambled to pick up the rifle and aim it.

The Jabberwock leapt onto the cab, landing on top of the flimsy windshield and crushing it. The un-tempered glass shattered, covering Patel and Densler in broken fragments. Patel screamed and clutched his face.

The demon clawed at the cab, trying to find a foothold as it tried to stay perched in such a precarious position. Densler finally was able to aim the AR-15 in the direction of the beast and he began to fire at its grossly misshapen head.

The bullets passed through it, removing small chunks of flesh each time one found its mark, but the fiendish monster failed to even acknowledge the wounds. Densler swung the rifle at the creature's head, but it caught the AR-15 in its huge mouth. It yanked the weapon out of Densler's hands and tossed it. Densler heard it *clank* as it fell into the rear cargo bed.

It turned its cadaverous head to Densler, who tried to back away much as possible. Densler lay back in the seat, almost down to the floor, but the creature's enormous head pursued him, aided by its serpentine neck.

Finally, with nowhere else to escape, Densler looked straight into the creature's tiny pinprick eyes. Its gruesome jaws were now only inches from Densler's head. It chattered its teeth at him, in what he now truly recognized as the creature's distinctive laugh.

THE DESERT

He stared at the monster and saw, in these last moments, something indescribably human behind the eyes. He understood with a strangely calming clarity that his grandfather's theory of the afterlife was correct. Indeed, the thing in front of him had been human once, and now because of the black cynicism of its soul, had since become something of an avatar of blind hatred and psychopathic evil.

At that moment, he no longer feared death because he knew that something wonderful awaited him on the other side. He was prepared for it and resigned to it. He laughed back in the creature's face.

It looked at him for a moment and then suddenly turned its head at an odd angle. The pinprick eyes that glowed so fiercely before now dimmed and became dull, colorless orbs. Then he heard and understood.

"Yeah, that's right, motherfucker!" said Patel. "Who's laughing now, you son of a bitch?"

Densler now noticed Patel's left hand wrapped around the neck of the beast, his right just finishing decapitating it with the Ka-Bar.

Patel grabbed the Jabberwock's severed head and tossed it out of the cab and in front of the vehicle. Then he kicked the limp, headless body off of the front of the UNIMOG. There was a slight lurch as the vehicle ran it over. The sergeant wiped the blade of the Ka-Bar and held it up to his face.

"I'm keeping this, Specialist," said Patel. "Got it?"

"Sure thing, Sarge," said Densler, still in a state of shock.

Chapter 85

The Desert. 27 October 2009. 2027 Hours.

"Sarge," said Densler. "You don't look so good."

"Speak up, son," said Patel, "my hearing's coming back, but I still can't hear you."

"I said you don't look so good."

"Yeah," said Patel. "I think my left eye is fucked."

Indeed, the sergeant's eye and much of the left side of his face was severely lacerated. Little shards of glass poked out of some of the wounds. The bandages on his right arm were soaked in blood. It had probably taken a Herculean effort to cut through the Jabberwock's neck, and Patel had suffered for it.

"Let me drive, Sarge," said Densler.

"No way," said Patel. "I'd have to take my foot off the gas, and I don't want to chance another stall. I'd like to slow down though, to save gas. I can't see shit right now. Damn blood is running in my good eye. Are we alone yet?"

Densler looked around. He didn't see any other creatures around them, but the green fog was still thick. Ahead, he saw

THE DESERT

the glimmer of something on the horizon, glowing brighter than anything else.

"I don't see any of them around," said Densler. "But up ahead, something is glowing really bright."

Patel slowed back down to around ten miles per hour. Fifteen minutes later, Densler could see better what lay ahead.

"No fucking way!" said Densler. "That's impossible!"

"What?" asked Patel. "What's impossible?"

"The village, Sarge," said Densler, defeated. "It's the goddamned, cocksucking village. We've done it again. We're going in circles."

Chapter 86

The Desert. 27 October 2009. 2221 Hours.

"There's no way," said Patel. "We've been driving in a straight line away from the village for two and a half goddamned hours. It's impossible."

"Maybe," said Densler. "But if you'd told me a week ago that I'd be fighting fucking demons and my commanding officer was going to get turned into a zombie, then I probably would have said that was impossible too."

"It still doesn't make any sense," said Patel.

"Why should it?" said Densler. "I'm gonna take the damned ropes off now so we can turn around and find some high ground for the night." He reached for the steering wheel.

"No!" yelled Patel. He pushed Densler away from the wheel. "Now I get it! Don't turn around. Ockham's fucking razor."

"Excuse me?"

"All things being equal, the simplest solution tends to be the best one."

THE DESERT

"And the simplest solution to you is to drive back to that village in the middle of the night?" asked Densler, a note of incredulity apparent in his voice.

"Listen," said Patel. "We've been driving in a straight line away from the village, right?"

"Yeah," said Densler.

"Okay, so logic would dictate that we can't possibly be heading back into the village, right?"

"Okay?"

"So maybe we're not heading right back into the village," said Patel.

"But it's right there!" said Densler. "I can see it quite plainly."

"Maybe you just think you do," said Patel. "Maybe, that's what we're supposed to think. Then, we turn around, and get more lost. That's probably what happened to Henson and Taylor. They kept running into the village and turning around, only it wasn't the village. It was just an illusion."

"And you're so damned sure of this that you're willing to bet our lives on it?" asked Densler.

"Yes," said Patel. "Indeed I am."

Chapter 87

The Desert. 27 October 2009. 2245 Hours.

"Sarge," said Densler. "We're a lot closer to the village now. I can see the details. It's crawling with Jabberwocks and all manner of monstrosities. We need to turn around."

"Densler," said Patel. "You've been through a lot tonight, so that's why I'm not gonna knock you right the fuck out right now. But still, don't push me."

As they neared the village, a new creature walked out towards them, larger than anything they had encountered so far. It stood in the middle of the front entrance, blocking entry to the village.

The monster was about eighteen feet tall and more humanoid than any of the other horrors they had yet seen. Surrounding it was a mist of coal black air that seemed to burn and smolder, and flecks of ash floated upon the air around it. When Densler tried to look directly at it, it was as if the creature was not completely visible. It was as if the creature could only be seen out of the corner of his eye, or with his eyes unfocused. The creature's head was not

THE DESERT

immediately visible as much of the monstrosity appeared to be cloaked in the mist. As soon as they were within about twenty feet of the demon, it raised its right hand, palm out towards the truck. Although the engine clearly still revved, suddenly the UNIMOG seemed to stop moving forward.

Oh great fucking idea, Sarge, thought Densler. *I guess this is the end. After all of the shit that I just went through, we serve ourselves up on a platter to the leader of the shitheads. Peachy.*

It lowered its hand, but the vehicle still ceased to move forward. Patel pushed his foot all the way down on the pedal, causing the engine to race loudly. Other creatures, Jabberwocks, gargoyles, shades, ghosts, and things that Densler had not seen before, came out from the village and surrounded the UNIMOG.

As Densler began to get the hang of looking at the creature askance, he saw that occasionally the fiend's head became momentarily visible. The creature's head was basically human. It looked neither male nor female and had no hair. Its skin was transparent, and the white skull beneath was plainly visible. Its eyes were also clear, like glass marbles, and there were no visible irises. It opened its mouth to speak, and when it did, Densler saw that its teeth were like those of the Jabberwocks, long, thin, clear spikes.

"*Alheirux!*" the creature said, in a voice that sounded like embers crackling in a fire. "*Alheirux vakta! Alheirux viktun!*"

The creature raised its left arm, and the hand became visible, only it was less a hand than a mass of tentacle-like appendages, wrapping around and among each other. The ropey, sinuous tentacles uncoiled from the arm, stretching down to the ground. The creature raised its hideous arm above its head, and the tentacles wove together into a single strand, resembling an enormous whip.

"Close your eyes, Densler," said Patel.

"What?" asked Densler.

"I said, *close your eyes*. It can't hurt us now. We're almost free."

"What do you mean?"

"Just do it, before I *do* knock you the fuck out."

Reluctantly, Densler closed his eyes.

The creature repeated its peculiar phrase, this time louder and more forcefully, *"Alheirux! Alheirux vakta! Alheirux viktun!"*

And then, there was only the sound of the truck, racing across the desert.

THE DESERT

Chapter 88

The Desert. 27 October 2009. 2319 Hours.

Densler opened his eyes. The village was gone. Ahead of him, the desert was dark, but not as dark as before. The moon shone faintly down upon them. Stars littered the sky above. And nowhere was there even the slightest tinge of green.

"You're shitting me," said Densler.

"I never thought I'd be so happy to see a clear Iraqi sky," said Patel.

"We could have left at any time," said Densler. "We could have driven away."

"No," said Patel. "You'd have just driven around in circles and run out of gas. Hell, I might have fallen for that shit if my eyes weren't so messed up. I still can't see much of anything."

"You have any idea in what direction we're going?"

"Not a clue," said Patel. "But now that we have a moment, would you mind telling me something?"

"Sure."

"What the hell were you and Henderson doing driving around in the middle of Iraq alone?"

"Looking for WMDs," said Densler. "I guess we found them."

"So I guess we won the war then."

"In a manner of speaking. I wouldn't say that it is actually possible to truly win a war anymore, though. Not if what you are trying to do is make the world a better place, at least. Only tyrants can truly win wars. Everyone else just tries to stop them from winning. At the end of the day, even if the good guys win, they've still lost."

"Are there any friendly bases around here, then?" asked Patel.

"There's an Army outpost somewhere in the vicinity," said Densler. "That's where we came from. We couldn't have driven more than twenty or thirty miles away before we got lost."

"Well then," said Patel. "Let's just hope we don't get lost. Now help me get these damned ropes off my steering wheel."

THE DESERT

Chapter 89

The Desert. 28 October 2009. 0254 Hours.

The MINIMOG sputtered and died. Densler and Patel were greeted by an unusually calming silence. Patel opened his door and slid down out of the front seat. He patted the hood of the truck.

"You did good," said Patel. "I'm sorry to have to leave you out here in the middle of nowhere."

"Eh," said Densler. "Some shepherd is gonna come out here and find this thing and it'll be like he won the Iraqi lottery. Don't worry about the old girl."

"Let's camp here for the night," said Patel. "I'm too tired to walk right now. I need rest."

Densler hopped into the rear of the cargo bed and sat down. Patel grabbed a flashlight and the UNIMOG's rear view mirror from the floor of the cab and sat down next to him. He then proceeded to start pulling the glass fragments from his face using the mirror and flashlight to see what he was doing.

"You want some help with that, Sarge?" asked Densler.

"Nah," said Patel. "Just see if you can find something for me to wrap my face up in. I don't want to keep bleeding into my good eye."

"You bet," said Densler. He went to the cab to look for more first aid supplies. When he returned, he could see that Patel was struggling to keep from crying as he removed the glass from around his eye. Then Densler realized that he was actually removing a piece of glass from his eye socket.

Jesus Christ, that guy is nuts, thought Densler. *What kind of Rambo shit is that, anyways? He can't let me help him remove the fucking glass from his eye? He'll be lucky if he doesn't pass out. I hope he'll be okay tomorrow. We may have a lot of walking around in the desert sun.*

Chapter 89

The Desert. 28 October 2009. 1256 Hours.

"Sarge," said Densler. "You really need to take some of this water. You've lost a lot of blood. I'm fine."

"So am I," said Patel. "I've survived for six years, constantly fearing for my life because of those goddamned demons, and I'm not going to let a simple thing like the damned *desert* do me in."

The two men had been walking since 0600 hours. At midday, the temperature was well over 110 degrees. They had seen no evidence of civilization since leaving the village the night before.

"Do you hear that, Sarge?" asked Densler.

"I don't hear much of anything, son," said Patel. "I can barely hear you."

"It sounds like an engine," said Densler. "Can you see anyone out there?"

"No," said Patel. "Wait. Over there, on the other side of that hill. Is that a dust plume?"

"Holy shit," said Densler. "I think you may be right."

Patel pulled out the UNIMOG's rear view mirror from his pocket and began angling it towards the vehicle, moving it around and hoping to cause it to glint from the sun. After a few moments, the vehicle appeared to turn towards them.

"It'll be a few minutes before whoever that is gets here," said Densler. "I wanted to talk to you about something."

"Sure," said Patel. "Go ahead."

"When we were heading towards the village," said Densler, "the illusion village, I mean. That thing that was standing there. Was it anything you'd seen before?"

"To tell you the truth, son," said Patel. "I couldn't see much of anything at that point. My good eye was all messed up because of the blood. I could hear a little something. Sounded like gibberish."

"Yeah," said Densler. "It talked."

"Of course," said Patel, "it was only an illusion."

"But an illusion of *what*?"

Patel shrugged.

"I think it was *him*," said Densler.

"Him who?" asked Patel.

"Hades," said Densler. "I think we met the lord of the fucking underworld."

"You didn't meet anyone," said Patel. "You saw an illusion."

"Are you sure?" asked Densler. "How can you be sure?"

"I'm as sure as I want to be," said Patel. "Don't you *want* me to be sure?"

As the approaching vehicle came closer, Densler could see that it was an American Humvee. He looked down at himself, noting the tattered, filthy remnants of his uniform. He tossed down his rifle and held up his hands.

"We're American!" said Densler. "Don't shoot!"

Chapter 90

The Desert, 29 October 2009, 0904 Hours.

"You expect me to believe this nonsense?" said the interrogator, an African-American E-6 staff sergeant. "Where is Captain Henderson, and who is this guy you brought with you? Which insurgent group is he working for? Al-Qaeda? Who?"

"I've told you before, Sergeant Crowe," said Densler, irritated and frustrated. "That's Sergeant Patel of Eight-Up Platoon. Captain Henderson is dead. We ran into this village..."

"There is no goddamned village!" shouted Crowe. "There's nothing out there where you're talking about! This is the most ridiculous cover story I've ever heard. You better start talking, or you're gonna end up somewhere a whole lot worse than Guantanamo Bay!"

Densler sighed. *At least they let me take a shower and get into some clean clothes,* he thought. *And boy was that shitty Army breakfast a welcome sight. Too bad we didn't think about this earlier. Patel and I should have come up with some sort of bullshit story, because they ain't buying the truth. That's for sure.*

Densler sat in a trey, windowless room. There was a brown fold-up table pushed to the side of the wall, and Densler sat in an uncomfortable plastic chair, wearing a clean, but unmarked, Army ACU uniform. He relaxed as well as possible, glad that he had had a reasonable amount of sleep the previous night.

Crowe paced around the room. He had another plastic chair facing Densler, but he had barely sat in it since he had entered the room. This was their second session. Densler had been brought to Crowe the previous afternoon.

Suddenly, there was a knock at the door. Crowe went to the door and a Specialist opened it. He leaned forward and whispered something in Crowe's ear.

"Well then," said Crowe. "It looks like one part of your story is true. I see that we've positively identified your partner in crime as Sergeant Mahabala Patel, missing in action and presumed dead, since the invasion."

"Good," said Densler.

"Now why don't you tell me what really happened to Fourth Platoon?" said Crowe, his voice now calm and quiet. He sat down in the plastic chair and leaned forward, towards Densler. "Are there any more of them out there? Are the insurgents holding them or did they execute them when Patel flipped?"

"Patel isn't a goddamned traitor!" yelled Densler. "And neither am I! This is bullshit!"

"I know you don't think of yourself as a traitor," said Crowe, still calm and quiet. "I'm sure you just did what you thought was right. Did you convert, or is this just about money?"

THE DESERT

"Neither!" said Densler.

"What *is* it about then, Hasil?" said Crowe. "Was it something you didn't like about Henderson? I hear he was a royal asshole. I'd have probably considered turning him over to the insurgents myself if I'd had to work with him everyday like you did. Come on, tell me what happened."

Chapter 91

The Desert. 31 October 2009. 1031 Hours.

"This is your last chance, Densler," said Crowe. "We've given you three days to tell us what really happened out there. Patel's already spilled the beans. He told us that you found out that he was working with the insurgents and he offered to pay you to deliver an officer. You didn't like Henderson, so it was a match made in Heaven."

"Patel didn't say that," said Densler. "You know goddamned well he didn't. That's a ridiculous story."

"Ridiculous?" asked Crowe. "No, what's ridiculous is this story of yours about...what were they again? Jabberwockies, demons, gargoyles, and even Lucifer himself? And then there's my favorite part—when Captain Henderson turns into a zombie and you blow both his arms off with your AR-15. You've already admitted to murdering Henderson. Now it's just the rest of the story I need to hear from you."

"You already have it," said Densler. "I'm not gonna make up some bullshit just to make your job easier."

THE DESERT

"So what then?" asked Crowe. "You're gonna keep telling the same nonsense story until we believe that the insurgents put some kind of *Manchurian Candidate* mumbo-jumbo on you? If that's your plan, then it ain't gonna work. You'll eventually tell us what we want to know, so you might as well say it now and spare yourself the trouble.

"And another thing," said Crowe. "Just because we stopped using certain...techniques...at Guantanamo Bay, doesn't mean they won't be used against you. We have secret places for treasonous bastards like you. Trust me. You won't last a week. Now tell me, what happened to Captain Henderson?"

"I'm not gonna waste any more time with you, Sarge," said Densler. "You obviously can't handle the truth."

"The truth," said Crowe, chuckling. "The truth is what I say it is, Soldier."

Chapter 92

The Desert. 31 October 2009. 1709 Hours.

"They'll be moving you out of here later tonight, Densler," said Crowe. "They like to do this sort of thing under the cover of darkness, you know. Don't expect to ever see a lawyer or a reporter, or frankly, anyone who gives a damn about you. You're gonna die there, Hasil."

"Better there than in that village," said Densler.

"So you say," said Crowe.

There was another knock at the door, this one very urgent. Crowe went to it, and a Major opened the door and pulled him out of the room. Densler could hear muffled shouting coming from the other side of the door. After a couple of minutes, the major opened the door and stepped inside, carrying a manila folder.

The major was a white guy, square-jawed and bulky. He looked to Densler more like Special Forces than Intel. His nametape identified him as Major McClendon. He sat down in the chair across from Densler.

"We found the UNIMOG," said Major McClendon.

THE DESERT

"Good," said Densler. "I don't suppose that means you've started believing what really happened out there."

"Not completely," said McClendon. "However, I'd like you to tell me what you can about what's in these photographs."

McClendon opened the manila folder and handed a set of eight by ten photographs to Densler.

"This was recovered from the undercarriage of the UNIMOG," said McClendon. "It appears to have become stuck there when you drove over it."

Densler looked at the photographs with astonishment. They were a series of photos of soldiers holding up something grotesque, pallid, and instantly recognizable to Densler. Although it had suffered a significant amount of damage, and parts of it had fallen away, it was quite obvious to Densler that the soldiers were holding the severed head of the chattering Jabberwock.

Epilogue

The Desert. 03 January 2010. 0611 Hours.

Command Sergeant Major Patel lowered his binoculars. He decided that after this was over, he was going to get a spyglass to replace them. He just felt that using binoculars was a bit ridiculous since he only had one eye now. He wore a black eye patch over the gaping socket. The doctors had suggested a glass eye, but Patel had declined, feeling that such a thing was akin to wearing a hairpiece to cover up a bald spot.

Patel stood looking out through the front hatch of his FCS *C2V* command and control vehicle. Ahead, the first rays of sunlight began to illuminate a small village in the distance.

Flanking his vehicle were a line of MCS, or *mounted combat system* light tanks, five on each side. Behind him stretched a line of tanks and artillery vehicles worthy of brigade-level strength.

"Sergeant Major," said the communications specialist below him in the vehicle, "all comms appear to be dead. I can't communicate with Major McClendon."

THE DESERT

"Don't worry about that, Specialist," said Patel. "We knew that would happen. Do you still have communications with the rest of the strike force?"

"No, Sergeant Major. All I get is this weird open channel and some scratching sounds and..."

"Okay," said Patel. "Shut off the radio then. I'll have to address them myself. I planned ahead for this."

Patel rummaged inside a rucksack near his feet and pulled out an olive drab painted bullhorn. He then climbed out of the vehicle and stood with his back to the village.

"Everybody shut your engines off so you can hear me!" shouted Patel.

After a few minutes for the word to get passed around, the desert became silent.

"Do not use your radios any more during this engagement," said Patel. "Keep them shut off. I want you all to listen to me now, because this is important. No matter what you see in there, stick to your orders. You may see some crazy shit, and I want you to be prepared. Our orders are to demolish the village and collapse the underground base. Hooahh?"

The desert echoed with the sounds of hundreds of soldiers replying, "Hooahh!"

"We tried to get the Air Force to do it for us, but they kept missing the target. Now it's our turn, understood?"

Again, the still desert silence was shattered by the soldiers' words of assent. Patel climbed back down into his command hatch.

You want Hell, you sons of bitches? he thought, *I'll show you Hell.*

He yelled into his bullhorn, "All vehicles, move out and engage your targets! Engage! Engage! Engage!"

About the Author:

Bryon Morrigan

Bryon Morrigan is a former military intelligence analyst with a degree in forensic science. He lives in a beautiful Southern estate in Florida with his wife and two daughters, where he is working on his next novel.

Printed in the United States
104124LV00003B/117/A